DECEPTIVE SHALLOWS

LANTERN BEACH EXPOSURE
BOOK 5

CHRISTY BARRITT

CHAPTER ONE

A FLUTTER of nerves felt more like kamikazes wreaking havoc inside Brandon Hale.

As thunder from a midsummer storm crashed overhead, he stared in the mirror set up in the Sunday school classroom at Lantern Beach Community Church. He readjusted his black bowtie and tried to push his apprehension away. He wasn't usually the nervous type.

A heavy hand came down on his shoulder. "You're not getting cold feet, are you?"

He glanced at Maddox King's image in the mirror.

His friend. His colleague. His best man.

Brandon shook his head before running his fingers through his short brown hair. "I have no doubt that Finley is the woman I want to spend the rest of my life with."

Maddox's eyes narrowed as he studied Brandon. "Then why do you look so apprehensive? You're never apprehensive."

Brandon turned toward his friend, his thoughts still racing. "I just have this bad feeling I can't put my finger on."

"Just because the fridge went out and the caterer had to scramble to purchase more food for the reception doesn't mean something else is going to go wrong." Maddox sliced his hand through the air as if it was settled. "Everything worked out, and your guests will now enjoy chicken fettuccine instead of shrimp scampi."

"Then the wrong flowers were put on the delivery truck, so now we have lilies on the stage instead of roses," Brandon reminded him.

"Not the biggest deal. Not really. I mean, Finley doesn't exactly seem like the bridezilla type."

"She's not. But—" Before he could finish his statement, another round of thunder rumbled. He pointed to the ceiling. "It's storming outside."

"Isn't that good luck on your wedding day?"

"I've never heard that one." His friend was just trying to make him feel better. "Thankfully, I don't believe in bad omens. Still, I can't shake this sense of foreboding."

"Your wedding is going to be perfect," Maddox said.

His friend's reassuring smile did make him feel better.

The rest of Brandon's groomsmen flooded into the room, each looking sharp in their tuxedos. But not as sharp as Maddox, who'd insisted on crocheting his bowtie.

It was a running joke in the group, and Brandon had almost asked him not to wear the tie. But Finley had insisted he should, that the piece added some personality to their event.

The photographer had already taken pictures of all the groomsmen together—but not of Brandon with Finley. He wanted to see her in her wedding gown for the first time when she walked down the aisle. He'd dreamed about this day for a long time.

At that thought, thunder clapped again, and rain began to batter the roof of the church.

As local musician Carter Denver began to play "A Thousand Years" on his guitar, Taryn Parsons—their wedding planner and Maddox's fiancée—appeared in the doorway.

Maddox let out a low whistle at the sight of her. Her cheeks flushed, and she quickly straightened his tie before turning to Brandon.

"It's time." Taryn smiled as she glanced at him. "You look handsome. I can't wait for you to see Finley. Make sure one of your groomsmen is close to catch you in case your knees buckle. Speaking of knees, don't lock them. Keep them slightly bent, you don't want to pass out."

He chuckled. "Noted."

With one more glance at his friends, Brandon stepped out of the classroom, down the hallway, and toward the sanctuary.

When he got the signal from Taryn, he stepped onto the stage, joined by Maddox, and his grooms-men, Dylan Granger and Rocco Foster.

The church was full, the guests mostly friends from Blackout as well as a few family members. The decorations were simple—two candelabras and those white lilies, which added a sweet scent to the air.

Brandon couldn't wait to get a glimpse of his bride. His beautiful, beautiful bride.

Finley Cooper was the smartest, most caring, most beautiful woman he'd ever met.

He had let her get away once, and he'd vowed never to do that again. Not by his own volition, at least.

The bridesmaids—Katie Logan and Peyton Ellison—started down the aisle, followed by Finley's childhood friend and maid of honor, Amanda Higgins, and then two-year-old Julia Dillinger, the flower girl. Everyone giggled as Julia paused once she reached the stage and bowed.

Everyone's attention startled the girl, and she ran to her mom and dad, who sat in the third row. They pulled her into their arms, grins on their faces.

As the song changed to "Can't Help Falling in Love," everyone rose.

Brandon's breath caught when he saw Finley standing at the end of the aisle, a soft grin on her lovely face. Her white, A-line gown highlighted her trim shoulders. Her wavy blonde hair was swept up in some kind of twist.

But it was her eyes he focused on . . . they were glowing. The sight of them brought him an intense satisfaction.

This was it. The moment he'd been dreaming about.

All those feelings about an impending storm were probably just nerves.

This was a big day. A big commitment. Even though Brandon had no doubts he wanted to marry Finley, something about planning the ceremony and all that had gone into it had clearly just messed with his mind.

He let out a breath and reminded himself to relax.

As soon as Finley stood in front of him and Brandon could feel her hands in his, everything would be okay.

But before she took the first step down the aisle, a commotion sounded in the distance.

As the hauntingly beautiful song floated through the air, Brandon stiffened.

Three men and a woman wearing dark suits

suddenly stepped from the foyer and surrounded Finley.

Alarm spread across his bride's face as gasps and murmurs traveled through their guests.

Brandon's heart kicked into overdrive. What was going on?

At once, the formalities of this moment didn't matter.

He rushed down the aisle toward Finley, desperate to see what was happening.

Especially when one of the men took Finley's arm.

"Hey! Get your hands off her," Brandon yelled across the sanctuary.

The man ignored his demand.

As the music abruptly ended, thunder crashed overhead.

Then Brandon heard, "Finley Cooper, you're under arrest."

———

Finley's world spun around her.

Before she could fully comprehend what was happening, her hands were cuffed behind her back.

A stony-faced FBI agent mercilessly led her from the sanctuary while the other agents followed.

Humiliation washed over her as she glanced back at everyone staring at her, mouths open with shock.

Her arrest put her on display in front of all the people who meant the most to her.

She couldn't believe this was happening.

Why *was* this happening? Surely, this had to be some mistake.

"Why are you arresting me?" She tried to dig in her heels, to stop this madness. It was useless. These men were stronger than she was. "Let me go! This is my wedding day."

"Unfortunately, certain things supersede a wedding," the humorless agent beside her said.

From the doorway, she glanced back, searching for Brandon.

All she wanted right now was to have him beside her.

As if on cue, he appeared. His blue eyes latched onto hers, concern filling them.

Momentary relief washed through her.

Everything was always better when Brandon was close.

But Finley wasn't sure that even he could fix this situation.

"What's going on here?" he demanded as he ran out ahead of them and held up his hands as if to block them.

A moment later, Colton Locke and Ty Chambers appeared beside him.

Three of the best Navy SEALs who'd ever been in

the business and an intimidating trio if there ever was one.

But the agents surrounding her were feds. They'd all flashed their badges at her at the same time, almost as if they'd rehearsed it. Right before one of them had grabbed her arm.

She had no doubt they meant business.

Finley had a feeling these feds wouldn't care about her friends' military status or that these men were capable of wiping out militias with the right strategic tactical plan.

A moment later, her assumptions were confirmed.

"You don't want to do this." The female federal agent walked straight for the wall of former SEALs as if she wasn't impressed. She flashed what Finley could only assume was an arrest warrant at them, and ordered, "Step aside."

They had no choice but to allow the feds to pass with Finley.

The agents led her outside, and rain soaked her. The downpour ruined the look it had taken hours to achieve. Drenched her wedding dress. Plastered her hair to her head.

Amanda joined them, still clutching her bouquet. Rain pelted her sea-glass blue-green dress. "Don't tell them anything, Finley! Ask for a lawyer."

Amanda was an attorney—and it seemed as if Finley might need a good attorney right now. Maybe a whole team.

"What are the charges?" Brandon asked as he kept stride alongside them.

"Treason," Stony Face said as he continued toward the dark SUV parked in front of the church.

"What?" Finley stumbled as she heard the word. "I would never . . ."

This *had* to be a mistake. She was no traitor.

"You have the right to remain silent . . ."

The rest of his words faded as apprehension flooded her.

Why in the world would she be arrested for treason?

Finley cast Brandon a glance, unable to hide the panic growing inside.

"We'll figure out what's going on," Brandon promised her as their gazes connected. "Stay strong. I know you didn't do this. We're going to prove you're innocent."

She knew he'd do everything in his power to do just that.

"I love you, Finley," Brandon called.

Emotion clogged her throat. "I love you too."

If she could just explain this was all a mistake . . .

But as soon as she looked at the FBI agents surrounding her, she knew there would be no reasoning with them. They already thought she was guilty.

She cast one more glance back at the open church doors and the sanctuary beyond.

Moments ago their guests had been anticipating celebrating the happiest day of Brandon's and Finley's lives.

Now, everyone gathered at the entrance looking horrified.

The white wedding dress Finley had meticulously picked out dragged through the mud in the gravel parking lot as she was shoved into the back of an FBI vehicle.

As she glanced at Brandon standing dumbfounded near the steps where people should be throwing bird seed at them later, the first tear rolled down her cheeks.

CHAPTER
TWO

BEFORE THE SUV left the parking lot, Brandon rushed back inside the church, bypassing the sanctuary and all the people waiting there. Instead, he darted down the hallway toward the classroom where he'd left his wallet and keys.

He needed to get out of here and follow Finley.

Maddox, Colton, and Ty were on his heels.

"Where do you think they're taking Finley?" Brandon called over his shoulder as he threw open the door to his temporary dressing room.

"To the police station to question her, if I had to guess," Ty said.

"Cassidy didn't say anything?" Brandon turned to look at Ty, to see his expression. His wife was the police chief, but she hadn't been able to attend the ceremony today because of some staff shortages.

Did his friend have any idea this would happen?

Brandon couldn't imagine that Ty did. Then again, he couldn't imagine any of this happening.

Ty shrugged. "I doubt she knows. With something like this . . . the feds don't have to give anyone a heads-up."

"I don't know what makes them think Finley could be guilty." Brandon grabbed his wallet and keys before rushing back out.

He nearly collided with Amanda in the hallway.

"What's going on?" A knot of confusion formed between her eyes, and her long, brown curls bounced as she looked back and forth between everyone.

"I have no idea," Brandon admitted.

Her frown deepened. "I'm not going to wait for them to let her call for an attorney. I'm going to the police station now."

"I'll give you a ride." Brandon started toward the back door when Colton placed a hand on his shoulder.

"Take a deep breath first. If you go in there hot, you're only going to make the situation worse."

Brandon still felt the flames shooting through his veins. As he slowly drew air into his lungs, lightning flashed again followed by thunder clapping overhead. In the distance, he could hear the murmur of guests as they talked amongst themselves.

All of this . . . it felt surreal.

"They said she was being arrested for treason."

Brandon tried to keep his voice down. "Do you realize how serious that is?"

He knew Colton understood—all his friends did. Brandon's words popped out anyway.

"Yes, I do." Colton's voice sounded even and calm. "They're obviously mistaken."

"How could they even think they have anything against her?" Brandon ran a hand through his hair, fighting the urge to begin pacing.

"I don't know, but they obviously have some kind of evidence if they got an arrest warrant. Brandon . . . those were feds."

His jaw hardened. "I know. This is not okay."

"I'll drive you to the station." Ty looked back at Colton. "Colton, can you handle things here? I'm sure the guests don't know what to do."

"Don't you worry about anything here at the church." Colton offered a confident nod. "I'll get with Taryn, and we'll handle it."

With that, Brandon and Ty hurried out the back door, Amanda at their heels.

He paused when he saw the limo parked outside.

"Just married" had been written in white letters on the back glass.

His heart panged with regret . . . and loss.

That foreshadowing he'd felt earlier today . . . he'd been right.

But Brandon had so desperately hoped he was wrong.

He paused as he glanced more closely at the vehicle through the downpour of rain.

The limo had a flat tire.

How was that even possible? Hadn't the driver noticed the flat? At that thought, he saw the driver in the distance, smoking near a patch of woods and no doubt wasting time until he was needed.

Brandon would deal with that later. Right now, he and Amanda climbed into Ty's truck. There were more important things to worry about.

Things like Finley.

Wasting no time, they headed down the road.

Brandon had to see her. He had to find a way to help her. But with her being in federal custody, his options were limited.

He would need to keep calm and think things through.

Meanwhile, he hoped Finley took Amanda's advice and didn't say anything to the feds without a lawyer present.

He knew they could twist anything she said and use it against her. Even saying something seemingly innocent could be detrimental to her case.

Somehow, he needed to prove that Finley wasn't guilty.

Brandon would find a way and do whatever it took to protect the woman he loved.

———

Finley struggled to hold back tears as the FBI agent pulled the SUV to a stop in front of the Lantern Beach Police Station.

As she was escorted inside, she spotted Police Chief Cassidy Chambers standing in the lobby. She wore a pensive, almost apologetic expression as she watched Finley being led to an interrogation room.

Finley's mind wouldn't stop racing.

Treason? She literally had no idea what the feds could be talking about. But she was about to find out.

The agents deposited her in a small room with a table shoved against one wall.

They had her sit in a chair at the table, one tucked into the corner farthest from the door. Probably to make her feel trapped. To intimidate her.

If so, it was working.

Only one agent remained with her. The man was tall with thick gray hair and a gaze that made him appear as if he could burn lasers into someone.

He removed her cuffs, and Finley drew her hands in front of her, rubbing her tender wrists.

Another agent quickly came inside and gave her a scratchy gray blanket to put around her shoulders. But nothing could ward off the chill she felt.

She left the blanket in her lap.

Then she shifted uncomfortably. Her cold, damp wedding dress formed a poof around her. Small tears and smears of dirt and mud marred the edges. Plus, her hair was wet and the tendrils that had escaped from her twist now clung to her face. Remnants of the rain slithered down her shoulders and cheeks.

She didn't bother to wipe the moisture away.

She'd searched for weeks for the perfect dress, and she'd settled on something simple with a scoop neck, fitted bodice, and flowing skirt.

Finding just the right one had brought her so much joy.

All of that seemed meaningless now.

Finley told herself to play this cool, that doing so would make her appear less guilty.

Despite that resolve, she rushed, "Why in the world have I been arrested?"

The agent—Reginald Bills, he'd said his name was—remained emotionless to the point where he almost seemed robotic. "You're the CEO of Embolden Tech, correct?"

"That's right," she said.

"Tell me more about your company." Agent Bills pressed his lips together as he waited for her answer. His stare seemed to indicate that one wrong move would solidify her guilt and seal her fate.

She thought of Amanda's warning not to say anything. But surely it wouldn't hurt to tell him what her company's mission was. It was public knowledge anyway.

"We make cutting-edge technology that we sell to the military and paramilitary organizations.

Cameras. Listening devices. Cell phone jammers. You name it."

"And how long have you been the CEO?"

"I took over about a year ago." These questions were safe enough to answer, right? They weren't asking her anything they didn't already know.

He was probably establishing a baseline for the interrogation. Asking her the easy questions first. Then he'd go in for the kill.

"My father started the company," she added.

The agent jotted some notes down. "Tell us about the deal you made with the Chinese government."

Finley's breath caught. "The Chinese government? There is no deal. My company doesn't deal with China at all."

"Are you sure about that?" Bills stared at her, his expression hard and unyielding.

"Positive."

Bills narrowed his eyes. He wasn't wasting any time, was he? So much for establishing any kind of rapport with her.

Maybe he didn't feel the need.

Which terrified her even more.

"We have evidence that proves you personally gave them access to the servers you set up for the facial recognition cameras we contracted your company to create for us."

Outrage filled her. "I would never do that!"

He leveled his gaze with hers. "We have evidence

that refutes your statement. There's been an extensive investigation to trace the origins of the leak. The trail led back to you. Because of your actions, six Army Rangers were ambushed and killed two weeks ago."

"What?" The question came out as a whisper.

"The intel the Chinese government received access to allowed them detailed knowledge about a top-secret mission the Rangers were on."

"How?" The question rushed out before she could stop it.

"For starters, China had access to these men's facial features. They were able to track them via satellite. Secondly, the system had microphones that are also used for security purposes. China was able to use those microphones to eavesdrop."

"What?"

"Members of the People's Liberation Army were ready and waiting for the Rangers," Bills continued. "The PLA set numerous bombs to stop them. You know the rest of the story. Don't act like you didn't know about this."

"I'm not acting. I didn't have any knowledge of this." Finley's head began to spin. The media had been filled with news about the attack—but she had no connection to what had happened. "I would never do anything like that! Never!"

"Money is a huge motivator." Bills still appeared unconvinced. "Even the most seemingly innocent will turn for the right amount of cash."

"What are you trying to say?"

"Stop with the innocent act. Did you really think that we wouldn't be able to find the hidden bank account you opened? That we wouldn't be able to trace it back to you? The one with the two-million-dollar deposit that went through two weeks ago—the day after the Rangers were ambushed."

Panic rose in her, and shivers overtook her body. But her tremors weren't from the cold—they were from a sense of despair that pressed on her lungs until she couldn't breathe.

"Someone's setting me up. I didn't take any money!"

"You're going away for a long time, Ms. Cooper. One day, your fiancé is going to thank us for stopping this marriage before it ever happened. Your life will never be the same—just like the families of those Rangers who died."

Her world continued to spin around her.

The feds were accusing her of selling US secrets to the Chinese government.

For two million dollars.

And of ultimately being responsible for the death of six American soldiers.

If people believed Finley was a traitor, she would become one of the most hated people in the country.

How could this have happened?

Was this some kind of huge mistake? Or was someone trying to frame her?

Who would hate her enough to do this?

"I'd like to talk to my lawyer." Finley crossed her arms, praying she hadn't already said too much. "I know my rights."

Agent Bills pushed a cell phone across the table toward her. "Go ahead."

She picked up the phone and dialed her friend's cell.

Amanda picked up on the first ring. "Hello?"

"Amanda . . . it's me. Finley."

"Finley! Are you okay?"

"I need you down here at the police station. Now."

"Ty, Brandon, and I are almost there. Don't say anything until I get in there with you."

It didn't matter what Finley said . . . these feds already had their minds made up.

As far as they were concerned, she was now an enemy of the United States.

———

Brandon, Amanda, and Ty arrived at the police station a few minutes later.

Amanda introduced herself to the agents standing guard in the lobby as soon as they walked inside and then she headed straight to the interrogation room.

Brandon wished he could go with her, but he knew he couldn't.

Instead, he'd have to wait for an update. Wait to hear how the FBI had made this egregious mistake.

His mind wouldn't stop racing as he walked toward Cassidy's office, with Ty in the lead. Ty barged inside.

Cassidy frowned up at them from her desk as Ty shut the door behind them.

Brandon was thankful to be away from the watchful glances of the FBI agents lingering in the lobby. They'd eyed him as if he might be an accomplice or next on their list of people to arrest.

"What's going on, Cassidy?" Brandon didn't bother to sit. He couldn't if he wanted to. He was too wound up.

She shook her head slowly. "I don't know. Even if I did, I'm not sure how much I could tell you. But the feds came in about an hour ago and told me they needed to use the station. They didn't say why. I had no choice but to let them. I was surprised to see them bring Finley in here."

"They're saying that she's guilty of treason."

"Treason? That's a serious charge." Her eyes widened. "You have no idea why they might say that?"

"No!" His voice rose, and he reminded himself to stay calm. "I mean, *no*. Finley wouldn't do anything like that."

"*I* know that. But why do the *feds* think she did?"

Brandon began pacing, running his hand through his hair.

He'd already taken off his damp jacket, discarded his bowtie, and undone the top buttons of his shirt. But he was still hot. Sweat covered his skin.

"I have no idea," he murmured. "How am I going to get her out of this?"

Cassidy handed him a bottle of water.

He took a long sip.

"Most likely she'll go before a judge, who will decide if bail will be set," Cassidy explained. "If they do set bail, then Finley should be able to return home . . . with some strict guidelines, of course."

"How long might that take?"

"It could be anywhere from twenty-four to seventy-two hours."

Brandon paused as the reality of the situation slammed into him. He rubbed a hand over his face. "I can't believe this is happening. And on our wedding day at that . . ."

"I'm so sorry." Cassidy's voice softened. "I truly am. Could someone have set her up for this? Either that or it's a misunderstanding?"

"It's one of those two. She is *not* guilty."

Cassidy nodded. "Has anything strange happened lately?"

"Everything that could go wrong with the wedding seems to have gone wrong. But really, it was all minor things until this happened. There were no serious red flags. No my-fiancée-might-be-accused-of-treason red flags."

"And Finley hasn't had any trouble at work lately?"

"No, I think she would have mentioned it."

Cassidy pressed her lips together in thought. "I wish I knew more. But I don't. Not yet. For now, there's nothing we can do until she goes before the judge—nothing but pray and wait for more information."

Brandon knew her words were true.

But he hated feeling so helpless.

CHAPTER
THREE

FINLEY'S LUNGS remained tight as she stood in front of the federal judge at the courthouse in Raleigh. She smoothed the white top and black pants Amanda had brought for her to wear.

Amanda had presented her case as to why Finley wasn't a flight risk.

She had no past criminal record, was an upstanding citizen who often helped with charity events, and she ran a successful company.

Would that be enough for the judge to grant her bail?

She wasn't sure.

Amanda had already prepped Finley for the possibility that her argument might not work. That the legal system may want to keep her in holding until her trial.

She prayed that wasn't the case.

Brandon was seated right behind her. He'd brought Dylan, Maddox, and Rocco with him.

US Magistrate Whitmore had already reviewed the charges against her: one felony count of conspiracy to communicate restricted data, and two counts of committing espionage on behalf of China. She faced life in prison.

Finley had pled not guilty.

She and Amanda stood right now, Amanda with her hair in a twist and wearing a black business suit, looking serious and determined. Finley tried to appear composed but wasn't sure she pulled it off.

"Ms. Cooper, I truly hope you're not guilty of this crime." Judge Whitmore stared down at her, his hook nose and wrinkled face seeming grandfatherly—even though he was apparently more of a shark than a teddy bear. "Because of your upstanding reputation, I'm going to grant you bail—in the amount of two million dollars."

Murmurs passed through the crowd behind her.

"Keep in mind you must adhere to the terms of your bail. You must abstain from drug and alcohol use. I'm also going to require you to turn over your passport and not leave the state of North Carolina. If you break the terms of this, then you will be remanded into custody and remain in prison until your trial. Do you understand?"

"Yes, your honor."

Judge Whitmore hit his gavel against the bench. "The bailiff will take you to begin the bail process."

Finley turned toward Amanda and threw her arms around her. Her friend had done a wonderful job spelling out why Finley was innocent—and they weren't even at trial yet.

"Thank you," Finley murmured.

"Of course."

As soon as she pulled away from Amanda, she glanced at Brandon.

The relief on his face was visible, and Finley wanted nothing more than to hug him also.

But she couldn't right now. Hopefully soon.

The bailiff—a big, burly man in his fifties—took her arm.

"We have everything lined up for bail," Amanda called. "Just give us a couple of hours, and we'll get you out of here."

Finley could pool her resources. Put her house on the line as well as her retirement funds. Then when she was found innocent, she would get that money back.

She had the past twenty-four hours of sitting in a holding cell to think all this through.

To ruminate on who may have set her up like this.

Because that was the only thing that made sense. That she'd been set up.

She had *not* sold any secrets to China. She would

never do that. She especially wouldn't have done something to put members of the US military at risk.

"We're going to get you through this, Finley," Brandon murmured behind her.

She cast him a grateful smile.

He'd stuck with her. She'd known he would. He was that type of man—a rarity in her experience. Once you found someone that priceless, you never let them go. They'd had their ups and downs, but now she couldn't imagine her future without him.

Before the bailiff escorted her back to her holding cell, Finley cast one more glance at Brandon and Amanda.

They were getting her out of here. She only wished this meant the nightmare her life had become was now over.

But she knew the biggest fight of her life was just beginning.

———

Brandon paced the lobby as he waited for Finley to be released.

Amanda sat in one of several gray leather chairs that were lined up against the wall and watched him.

"Why don't you sit?" She patted a chair beside her.

He let out a breath, about to refuse. Instead, he nodded and plopped down two seats away from her.

When he glanced through the glass doors in the distance, he could see the crowds gathered there.

The FBI had given a press conference about Finley's arrest, and it had unleashed a firestorm.

He wasn't sure Finley would be prepared to deal with the public's interest—and outrage—about the crimes she was charged with.

But they'd cross that bridge when they got there.

"What's the plan after she's released?" Brandon asked, even though he was pretty sure they'd already talked about this.

"She needs to follow the conditions of her bail. I'm sure she won't have a problem doing that. She'll have to report back to the judge to ensure she's staying on track, and they'll eventually set a date for the trial."

"How far out?"

"It could be a few months. This is a big case. I'll probably need to bring in some of my partners to help with things. I've never handled charges of this magnitude."

"If she's convicted?"

Amanda frowned. "Then she'll go away for life."

Brandon bristled. He couldn't let that happen. "Do you think they have enough evidence to convict her?"

She tilted her head, her expression pensive. "It's hard to say at this point. The feds claim to have emails. And the money in her account . . ."

"We have to prove she didn't set up that bank account."

Lines stretched across her forehead. "That's going to be difficult, but I'll do my best. The banks should have a record of it, but I'm sure the person who set her up has covered their tracks. And since you can do it online . . . they'll need to trace the IP address."

"I have a feeling it's going to lead back to Finley."

Amanda's frown deepened. "Me too."

"Whatever I can do to help you, let me know . . ."

The past twenty-four hours had been miserable. He'd rushed to Raleigh so he could be close in case Finley needed him. But he hadn't been allowed to talk to her. To hold her.

He'd wanted to jump in. To investigate.

But with so little information to go on, he'd had no choice but to wait and speculate.

Thankfully, his friends had been with him the whole time.

They'd looked into the death of those Rangers who had been killed. Had looked into the Chinese leaders Finley had supposedly been in contact with.

The Rangers had been on a mission to rescue a US businessman who'd been arrested in China on false charges. The government had attempted to use him as a bargaining chip. But as soon as the Rangers had moved into the compound to attempt the rescue, bombs had exploded.

Six men had died. Four had survived.

The tragedy had been all over the news as people mourned their loss.

Brandon and his team did all the research they could so they could be prepared for the fight ahead.

Now he needed to talk to Finley and find out who might want to do this to her.

He'd even talked to some of her coworkers and tried to find out who her enemies might be.

But no one had been able to name anyone.

Right now, Brandon just wanted to see Finley.

How much longer would this take?

CHAPTER
FOUR

THREE HOURS LATER, Finley was out on bail.

As soon as she was released from her holding cell and led into the lobby of the federal courthouse, she spotted Brandon. He popped to his feet when she emerged and quickly strode toward her.

He'd never looked more handsome.

In three steps, she reached him and threw her arms around him.

He pulled her close.

If Finley had her way, she'd never let go. She was fairly certain that Brandon felt the same way as tight as he squeezed her.

His strong arms and the familiar scent of his leathery cologne brought her a momentous sense of comfort.

But the feeling was short-lived when she heard something in the background.

It almost sounded like . . . chants.

Finley stepped away from Brandon and glanced back and forth between her fiancé and best friend.

"It's a zoo out there." Amanda explained as she nodded toward the door. "Reporters have been calling me nonstop wanting to get a quote from you."

"The media knows about this?" Finley's mind raced. "How did this information even get leaked?"

"The FBI held a press conference to keep the public informed. It's typical in situations like these."

Finley closed her eyes at Amanda's pronouncement. Of course.

Now the whole world thought she was guilty.

"We have an SUV waiting out back for you." Brandon kept a hand on her arm as if afraid she might get away again. "Maddox is driving, and we have four Blackout agents here to help hold back the crowds."

Her gaze locked with his. "It's that bad, huh?"

His brief nod was all the answer Finley needed.

Her company would be ruined, wouldn't it? All because of some false allegations.

Someone had linked her computer with the source of that leak. No doubt the FBI had that computer in their custody now and were analyzing her every keystroke from the past several months.

She'd heard the FBI had found a hidden email account with correspondence between Finley and

Muchen Weng, a high-ranking Chinese government official.

Then there was that money that had been placed into an overseas account under her name.

She'd never known it existed.

There was so much on the line right now. More than just her future. More than Brandon's future.

Embolden Tech was her father's legacy. What they did was important. The technology they developed was innovative and top-of-the-line.

Plus, Finley had more than two hundred employees working for her. If her company folded, they'd all be out of jobs.

Someone had shared US secrets that had gotten soldiers killed.

She couldn't think of anything more vile that a person could do.

Whoever was behind this needed to be stopped.

"Let's get you out of here." Brandon draped his arm around her shoulders, almost as if sheltering her from an oncoming storm.

Finley nodded and tried to brace herself for whatever she would encounter beyond the walls of this courthouse.

Yet another part of her knew there was no way she could prepare for whatever loomed ahead.

No one could.

———

Brandon wished he could spare Finley the pain of this situation. That he could snap his fingers and make her troubles disappear.

But that wasn't realistic.

He thought when Finley had been arrested that it had been the worst possible day of his life. But he realized this could get a lot worse.

Especially if Finley were found guilty.

People didn't take kindly to those they believed were traitors. He'd already seen uncountable comments about Finley online. Had heard the things people were chanting outside the courthouse.

They'd been nasty. People didn't think she deserved to live—to live free, at least. They'd mentioned things they'd like to do to her, things like killing her the way those soldiers had been killed.

Emotions ran high right now, and that made this situation even more dangerous.

As they reached the exit, Brandon braced himself for what was about to be unfurled onto Finley.

Titus, another Blackout operative, waited for Brandon's nod before opening the door.

As soon as he did, the crowd became amplified.

His only comfort was knowing his guys were holding back those gathered outside. That his friends had made a path for them.

"Are you ready for this?" Amanda turned toward Finley.

"As ready as I'll ever be." She drew in a shaky breath.

Brandon handed her some sunglasses and a baseball cap to conceal her face. Then he tightened his arm around Finley as he led her outside.

Despite the human shield Blackout provided, the crowds pressed in. They yelled over each other until nothing could be clearly understood. Cameras flashed. Microphones were shoved at them. Someone even volleyed a cup of soda toward them.

Thankfully, the liquid missed them.

Brandon rushed with Finley to the SUV. He shoved her into the back seat before climbing in behind her and slamming the door. Amanda climbed in beside the driver, while the other Blackout members flooded inside another SUV in front of them.

A moment of calm filled the vehicle as soon as the doors shut.

But Brandon knew it wouldn't last long.

Because the crowds surrounded the car. Rocked it. Practically consumed it.

They were facing multiple dangers right now—from the person who'd set Finley up to those who wanted her to pay for something she hadn't done.

CHAPTER
FIVE

PANIC BEGAN to bubble inside Finley.

As people surrounded their SUV, her lungs tightened until she felt as if she couldn't breathe.

What if they broke a window?

If they pulled out a gun?

If they refused to move?

These people wanted to make her pay for a crime she didn't commit.

"I've never seen anything like this," Amanda muttered as she glanced out the window.

The words didn't make Finley feel any better. The scope of what she was facing right now . . . it was overwhelming. The charges against her were horrific.

If someone had sold secrets to another country and innocent people had died because of it . . . then there was a reason to be angry.

But Finley had nothing to do with it.

Brandon squeezed her hand, pulling her from her negative thoughts. "It's going to be okay."

His steady voice always had a way of soothing her.

But Finley was having trouble seeing how this situation would be okay.

"Here we go." Maddox eased the car forward.

"Aren't you afraid of hitting someone?" Finley stared at the angry mob in front of the SUV.

"They'll move out of the way," Brandon assured her. "Local police are helping."

Her heart thudded into her chest. How could he be so sure?

It was only then that she noticed some of the signs people were holding.

Traitors should die.

An eye for an eye!

Death penalty for treason.

We don't want you here. Move to China.

Finley was supposed to be on her honeymoon right now. She and Brandon had been planning to go to the Maldives, where they had rented a cabana located on a pier over the clear turquoise water. They were going to spend a week basking in the sun and basking in each other.

Now, here she was.

Finley usually tried to stay positive. To keep her head upright. But she was struggling not to sink into the depths of despair right now.

She thought about telling Maddox to take her somewhere off-grid. The thought of hiding away from everyone was tempting.

But time wasn't on her side right now. Proving herself innocent would demand everything she had.

Maybe more.

Determination hardened inside her, and she straightened. "I need to go to the Embolden Tech headquarters. I need to try to figure out what's going on."

"Isn't there someone else at the office who can do it for you?" Amanda stared at her with concern in her gaze. "The fewer public appearances you make, the better."

"This is something I need to do myself. Especially until I know who I can trust."

Because Finley had to wonder if someone at the company had framed her.

She didn't want to think that could be true.

But that explanation made the most sense. Who else would have access to the information needed to make her look guilty?

"There are probably going to be crowds outside your office also," Brandon told her.

Her chest tightened. Of course. Why wouldn't there be?

But she still needed to get inside. The building itself would be secure. They had guards at the entrances, so reporters and protesters shouldn't be able to sneak inside.

As they pulled away from the courthouse, Finley glanced around her at the throngs of people. They still raged behind her. A few even chased after the vehicle.

Her throat went dry at the sight of them.

These people were out for blood—her blood— weren't they?

————

Just like at the courthouse, an angry mob picketed outside Embolden Tech's headquarters. The company was housed in a six-story building on the outskirts of downtown Raleigh.

And people were making their opinions known, Brandon mused.

As they pulled up to the side door, the crowds followed, seeming to know that Finley was inside the dark SUV.

Working quickly, Brandon ushered Finley from the vehicle. As soon as they stepped out, cameras flashed. Microphones were thrust into her face as reporters tried to get sound bites.

It was a madhouse.

Brandon got her through the crowd and inside. Amanda had decided to wait in the SUV and make some calls. Meanwhile, Maddox would circle the area.

Waiting outside would only spell trouble.

Brandon let out a sigh of relief once they got inside, behind locked doors.

The feeling didn't last long. They might be away from the scrutiny of the crowds, but Brandon knew Finley would be facing judgment from her employees also. Many of them were probably loyal to her, but there would be others who questioned her innocence, who wondered if she was a traitor.

As soon as they reached the sixth floor, Ron Winslow, one of the company's vice presidents met her. He'd been at the wedding, along with several other colleagues. Brandon thought the guy seemed nice enough.

"Finley . . . we didn't expect you to come here." He paused, shifting awkwardly.

The man was in his forties, with thick dark hair, a pointed nose, and a thin build. He was the Vice President of Operations, and he'd been on the job for the past six months after the man previously holding the position had been murdered. Finley had hired him herself. Brandon remembered her talking about it.

She continued past him toward her office. "I have to figure out what's going on."

"Finley." His voice held a somber tone.

Finley paused and turned toward him. "Yes?"

"The board . . . we had an emergency meeting last

night." He swallowed hard enough that his Adam's apple bobbed up and down.

Brandon realized where Ron was probably going with this and braced himself for the emotional impact of whatever the man was about to say.

"Okay . . ." Finley stared at Ron.

"I know this isn't what you want to hear, but the best thing we can do right now to salvage this company is to put you on a temporary leave of absence." Ron stared at her as he waited for her reaction. "It's not what any of us want, but given the circumstances . . ."

Fire lit in her eyes, and her hands went to her hips. "Temporary leave of absence? I'm the CEO of Embolden Tech. This is *my* company!"

Ron shifted. "No one wants to have anything to do with us. The government has canceled their contracts. Our stock has dropped nearly 25 percent."

Realization rolled over Finley's expression.

Certainly, she had to know this would happen. Then again, she'd had a lot to think about over the past couple of days. Business may have been one of the last things on her mind.

Finally, Finley licked her lips and nodded. "I understand. However, I need to get a few things from my office first."

Ron shifted, at least having the decency to look embarrassed about the conversation. "You do realize you can't take any proprietary information with you or any files."

Brandon glanced around and saw several people in the office watching them from their desks with curiosity. It was human nature, he supposed. Still, hadn't Finley been humiliated enough?

He knew Finley was innocent, and he hated that she was in this position. He hated that her reputation was on the line.

"Fine." She offered a tight nod. "Let me just grab some personal items."

Ron started walking beside her.

Finley raised her hand, her eyes narrowed with irritation. "I can do this myself."

"I'm sorry, but I'm going to need to watch you."

Another flash of testiness flickered in her gaze before quickly disappearing. "Fine."

Brandon understood why Ron was doing what he was. But none of this was fair.

Then again, life wasn't fair.

There were very few certainties concerning the future.

And Finley was again being reminded of that fact.

CHAPTER
SIX

AS LEADER OF EMBOLDEN TECH, Finley didn't like to show weakness. Being in charge was a delicate balance of calling the shots with unwavering confidence while also maintaining humanity and relatability.

Right now, tears pressed at her eyes.

She couldn't believe this was happening.

She had to stay strong. To keep her chin up.

She could fall apart later.

Unfortunately, she needed some of the proprietary information in her office if she wanted to figure out what was happening.

But as she stepped inside what used to be her haven, she felt Ron's watchful gaze on her. He was like a warden waiting for a prisoner to escape or to pull a knife.

She wasn't exactly sure how she would get what she needed with him watching.

She'd need to figure out a plan.

She grabbed some pictures of her dad she kept on a shelf in her office and a music box he had given her. Then an appointment calendar. She kept one on her phone also, but she liked to see her schedule in writing laid out in front of her.

Without moving her head, she peered up and saw Ron watching her every move.

Her jaw tightened.

What she really needed was a file she'd been working on recently—one that could hold answers. But how would she get it without Ron seeing her?

Brandon glanced at her, seeming to read her mind. He sprang into action.

"You're going to want to take this too, right?" He strode across the room toward one of the awards she had hanging on the wall.

As he did, Ron followed him with his gaze.

Finley quickly slipped the folder into the calendar. The pages concealed it perfectly.

Just in time.

Ron looked back but didn't seem to notice she'd done anything.

She released her breath.

Just as she shoved everything into an oversized leather bag she kept in her cabinet, an explosion rocked the outside of the building.

She glanced at the window as a ball of fire filled the air.

Brandon pulled her away, his body shielding hers.

Her heart pounded in her ears.

Someone was trying to recreate—right outside her office—what had happened to those soldiers.

They were not only trying to teach Finley a lesson but the whole company.

————

Things were escalating. Quickly. Too quickly.

Brandon planted Finley far away from the window—and directed Ron to move toward the hallway also.

A bomb had been set off outside.

Had someone taken things that far to drive home their point?

The good news was that the blast hadn't been powerful—probably from a small pipe bomb or something.

Brandon pressed his phone to his ear as he called Maddox. He needed to make sure everyone on the ground was safe.

Maddox answered on the first ring. Brandon could hear the crowds and sirens in the background.

"We're fine, but it's getting rowdy. The local

police really need to get involved with this. It's becoming a matter of public safety."

Brandon's jaw tightened. "I had no idea it would get out of hand like this. I need to get Finley out of here."

"We need to get the police here first." Maddox's voice was nearly drowned by the sound of the crowd around him. "The mobs of people out here are growing—not only in size, but in the level of their agitation."

Brandon stared outside, careful not to get too close to the window.

That was no peaceful protest out there.

Those people were out for blood.

CHAPTER
SEVEN

FINLEY WAS USED to calling the shots. To being the boss.

But she was too exhausted to do any of that.

Originally, she'd hoped to go back to Lantern Beach, but Brandon had said it was too much of a risk right now since people would expect that.

He seemed to think that things might calm down eventually. But what if that wasn't the case? How long would it take until people forgot what she'd been accused of doing?

What if they never forgot?

What if these false accusations became her legacy?

The questions all swirled in her head as they drove down the road. She and Brandon had success-fully gotten out of her office building, and they were all now headed away from Raleigh. Just as before,

Maddox was behind the wheel and Amanda sat in the back with them.

But no one seemed to know what to say.

What *did* one talk about in a situation like this?

Finley's own thoughts felt too heavy.

She wasn't even sure what direction they were going, and she didn't ask. She trusted Brandon.

She'd seen him glance out the back window several times, no doubt making sure no one was following them. She'd also felt Maddox take some sharp turns as they'd left the downtown area.

"Amanda picked up some clothes for you from your place, by the way," Brandon murmured. "The bag she packed for you is in the back."

"Thank you."

"Of course," Amanda said.

Then she frowned, and Finley knew something else was wrong. "What is it?"

Amanda let out a long breath. "When I went to your house . . . someone had spray-painted the front of it."

"What did they paint on my house?" Finley rushed.

"You can imagine what words they used . . . traitor and . . ."

"And what?"

Amanda's apologetic gaze met hers. "And . . . you deserve to die."

The blood drained from her face, though she shouldn't be surprised.

She was the most hated woman in the country right now.

Brandon kissed the top of her head. She leaned into him, still hoping this was simply a nightmare she'd wake up from, even though she knew it wasn't.

"What did you pick up from your office?" Brandon asked.

She reached into her bag and pulled out her calendar. Opening it, she grasped the file. "It might be nothing. But this is a list of our most recent clients, orders, and projects. I'm sure I've been locked out of Embolden's servers as a security precaution. But this will help me remember everyone we've worked with and what they've ordered. There's also an employee list. I was just reviewing it a couple of days ago. It had been on my list of things to do, and I wanted to mark it off before the wedding."

"It could come in handy. We can talk about that more when we arrive where we're staying tonight."

"Sounds good." She yawned. "If you don't mind, I need to rest for a few minutes."

"Take all the time you need."

She rested her head on Brandon's shoulder.

When she woke up, they were pulling through the gates of a massive mountain estate. Finley's eyes were glued to the window as the stone-faced house came into view. The place was sprawling and beautiful with immaculate landscaping.

"This is Taryn's place," Brandon told her.

"This is?" She'd heard part of Taryn's story, but she'd never imagined this.

"She inherited it after her boss passed."

"It looks amazing." Finley squinted. "Is that a labyrinth back there?"

"It is. In other circumstances, I'd say you should explore it."

In other circumstances . . . in other circumstances, Finley would be in the Maldives right now.

"You should be safe here for a while," Brandon continued. "I kept an eye on the road. No one was following us, and this place is secluded enough that no one should stumble upon it accidentally."

Finley couldn't wait to get inside.

She would shower and change, then get something to eat and drink some coffee.

Then they needed to spell out all the potential suspects.

Finley had a few in mind . . . but she had a hard time thinking that anyone hated her enough to go to these extremes.

But someone did.

And she needed answers.

———

An hour later, Brandon, Finley, Amanda, Dylan, and Maddox all sat around the kitchen table with full bellies. If only food could make the air of uneasiness around them disappear.

But it wasn't that easy—even if the deep-dish pepperoni pizza and cheesy breadsticks had been delicious.

"We've got to figure out who is doing this to you." Brandon turned toward Finley, ready to get down to business.

He'd been delaying discussing who might be guilty, trying to give Finley a breather. But this conversation couldn't wait any longer.

They all shifted into more comfortable positions. Maddox pulled out a skein of yellow yarn and his crochet hook. He started a chain of stitches, a tactic he used when trying to sort his thoughts.

"Yes, we do need to talk—to really talk." Finley frowned and pushed her plate away. "I've been thinking about this a lot. Whoever is responsible had to know about this tech and how it works. They would need to be skilled enough to be able to manipulate the data. There aren't many people who fit that description."

"Let's spell out exactly what happened," Brandon said. "Approximately a week before the Rangers employed a strategic mission to rescue someone from China, the Chinese government discovered their plan and then ambushed our troops."

"Correct." Finley frowned.

"Sometime before that, someone sold the Chinese the technology needed to eavesdrop into highly classified conversations using the facial recognition software. They did this by using technology developed by Embolden."

"Correct," Finley said again.

"After the Rangers were killed, US officials began looking for a leak—and that led them to Embolden's technology. They then began to investigate Embolden's employees, and that's when they discovered a secret bank account recently set up overseas in your name."

"Also correct."

"So whoever is behind this knows about the technology, how to use it, and how to get the information needed to set up that bank account."

"That about covers it."

"Do you have any ideas who might have done this?" His gaze met Finley's.

She let out a long sigh. "I've had a lot of time to think about this. And while I hate to point the finger at anyone, I do have a few best guesses."

Brandon grabbed a pad of paper from a bookbag he'd brought with him into the room. "Lay them out, and let's dig into each one."

She licked her lips before beginning. "First, there's Talen Schultz. He and my father were business partners, but they split ways when my dad started Embolden fifteen years ago. My dad said they had different visions for the company."

"What happened to Mr. Schultz?" Dylan asked.

"Embolden thrived while Talen's business folded after a few years. The few times I've encountered Talen, he still seems to have a chip on his shoulder. And he knows the tech world."

"We'll look into him." Brandon scribbled Talen's name on his paper. "Who else?"

Finley took a long sip of water before continuing. "Then there's Ryan Hold. He was one of our engineers, and he was brilliant. I hired him eight months ago. At first, he was great. Then he started acting peculiar."

"How so?" Amanda asked as she picked a piece of pepperoni from her pizza.

"He got mad easily," Finley said. "He even threw a tape dispenser at his assistant once because a misunderstanding caused him to miss a meeting. After that, we offered to pay for him to get the help he needed—some mental health treatment including anger management. But he refused. That was four months ago. We had no choice but to let him go. He was so angry with us because of it."

"Definitely sounds like someone we should check out." Brandon wrote down his name also. "Anyone else?"

She hesitated before finally saying, "Maybe Victor Newman."

"Who is Victor Newman?" Something about the way Finley said the man's name raised red flags.

She stiffly raised a shoulder. "He's a business analyst I went on a couple of dates with . . . back before you and I reconnected."

Brandon narrowed his eyes. "I don't remember hearing about him."

"One of my coworkers set us up. My brief relationship—if that's what you'd call it—with him seemed inconsequential . . . until about a month ago."

Brandon was liking this story less and less. "What do you mean?"

Finley let out a long breath. "I mean . . . when we went out a couple of years ago, I think he really liked me. But I wasn't really interested. When I told him I didn't want to see him anymore, he seemed offended. I had the feeling he liked to get his way."

"So what happened a couple of months ago?" And why hadn't she told him about any of this before? Brandon kept that question silent, not wanting to add any more stress to the moment.

"He showed up at the office and asked me to dinner. It was so out of the blue. I told him I was engaged, and he looked not only offended but angry. I didn't understand his reaction. Later, he sent me a scathing email, accusing me of leading him on. I ignored it . . . until now."

"I'm surprised you didn't mention this earlier, especially since you said you hadn't dated anyone since Ecuador." He clearly remembered her saying that. The fact that she'd kept this from him didn't seem like Finley.

Her gaze met his. "I didn't tell you because it just really seemed like a blip in the middle of everything else, not like a recurring problem. Besides, you were on an assignment out in California and . . ." She shrugged. "Maybe I should have mentioned it. I'm sorry."

"It's okay." Brandon trusted Finley's judgment. Right now, he needed to focus on more important matters. He stared at the three names on his list. "I'd say this is somewhere we could start. We can divide up the names, look into alibis, etc."

"Just tell us what you need us to do." Dylan straightened as if waiting for an assignment.

Brandon would have his colleagues look into these guys. Find out their whereabouts. If possible, maybe even look into their finances.

Because the person who'd done this either had to be a tech genius himself or he had the money to hire someone to do something like this.

It shouldn't be too hard to narrow it down . . . yet Brandon had a feeling it would be.

CHAPTER
EIGHT

FINLEY FELT her eyelids growing heavy as she sat at the table brainstorming ideas about why a person would go to such extremes.

There was hatred and then . . . there was *hatred*.

This was more than an online smear campaign or spreading gossip.

This person had set Finley up to go to prison for the rest of her life.

In her line of work, it wasn't unusual to be a target.

But she'd never imagined anyone taking things this far.

Brandon stood and rolled his shoulders back. "We need to take a break until morning. It's been a really long day."

Finley flashed him a grateful smile. He'd always been good at reading her—good at taking care of her.

She knew he must feel enormous pressure at the gravity of this situation.

Amanda stood, pulled off her glasses, and ran a hand over her face. "You're right. We could all use a break and some sleep right now. I can feel a headache coming on."

"We don't want that," Brandon told her.

"If you don't mind, I'm going to run upstairs for a long shower and turn in for the evening." Amanda stifled a yawn. "We can start fresh in the morning."

"Of course," Brandon murmured.

Finally, everyone filed from the room until it was only Brandon and Finley.

He took her hand and led her into an adjoining living room. There, he pulled her onto the couch beside him and wrapped his arms around her.

She melted in his embrace.

"You probably haven't slept since you were arrested, have you?" he murmured in her ear.

"No. I mean, maybe I drifted off a few times, but nothing substantial."

"I'm so sorry you're going through this."

"Me too." Her thoughts wandered. "What I wouldn't give to be on our honeymoon right now."

"You and me both."

"All of our friends at the wedding . . . what must they think of me?"

"Your true friends know you're innocent of this."

Finley knew Brandon's words were true. And she

wasn't usually given to being overly concerned about what people thought of her.

But her arrest had been mortifying.

"Sometimes, I feel like God really must not like me." Finley wasn't sure where the words had come from. They'd left her lips unchecked.

At the same time, she knew they were true. She'd been struggling with the thought for a while now.

She hated to admit it out loud, especially since she'd always felt fairly strong in her faith.

But not right now.

Brandon squeezed her hand. "Of course, He likes you. He *loves* you."

She wiped a stray tear. "I know. I mean, I *think* I know. But first, I lost my mom, then my dad was under suspicion, then he died, and someone tried to kill me so they could take over the company . . ." She shrugged. "It's a lot—enough heartache to last several lifetimes. I know some people who are my age who've never lost anyone, who've skated through life."

"I know it's difficult. But the strongest, most influential people of faith have often walked through the fire. That's how they've grown so strong."

"Maybe I don't want my faith to grow stronger." She frowned. "I probably sound immature. I'm just so tired."

"You've been through a lot. Just give yourself some grace and some time."

"What if this is it?" Her voice caught, and she glanced up at him. "What if the rest of my story is meant to take place behind bars?"

He pulled her closer. "Don't think like that."

"How can I not? What if we can't figure out who's behind this in time?"

Brandon laced his fingers through hers. "We will. You basically have everyone at Blackout at your disposal right now."

She knew those guys were the best of the best. And Amanda was a great lawyer. Even Katie Logan, Dylan's girlfriend, who was an award-winning investigative journalist, had offered to help. Katie could get Finley's real story in front of hundreds of thousands of readers.

But it was too early for that. They needed more answers before they went public with anything.

Finley found it comforting to know that a lot of people were rooting for her, and she had a support system. When both her parents had died, she'd felt utterly alone. Thankfully, things had turned around.

She also had a lot of people who'd love to see her demise, it appeared.

At that thought, her phone buzzed, and she glanced at the screen.

The words there caused her blood to grow cold.

You deserve all of this.

The person who'd done this to her had sent this . . . Finley was sure of it.

And now he'd sent this message to gloat.

Indignation—along with fear—shot up her spine at the realization.

But as quickly as the message had appeared, it was gone.

Finley blinked as she searched her texts.

But those words were nowhere to be found.

———

"What is it?" Brandon rushed as he heard Finley gasp.

"I got a message . . ." She held up her phone, a knot of confusion on her brow. "But now it's gone."

"What do you mean? Messages don't just disappear."

"I know." She tapped her screen several more times. "But this one did. It's as if I never got it."

Was this some type of new tech? It wouldn't surprise him. In fact, it almost seemed like something Finley's company might develop.

"What did it say?"

"It said, 'You deserve all of this.'" Finley frowned, still staring at her phone and shaking her head. "But without having any record of this message even coming through, it's going to be really hard to trace where it might have come from."

Brandon's back muscles pulled so tightly they felt like they might snap. "The person behind this is smart. I'm sure they didn't leave a trail anyway."

She shook her head before pinching the skin between her eyes. "You're probably right."

"Has Embolden developed any tech like this?"

"No, we haven't. And I haven't heard that any of our competitors have either—not that they would advertise it." She let out a long breath. "I just can't believe this."

"I'm not sure having your phone with you is safe," Brandon said. "What if someone traces it?"

"This phone is untraceable. It uses Embolden's technology. No one should be able to find me via the normal routes."

His jaw tightened with a touch of skepticism. He'd seen too many things in his time as a SEAL and then working for the CIA. He'd met too many slippery people.

But he would let this go.

For now.

Brandon's thoughts percolated as a better picture of the person behind these crimes came into his mind.

Brilliant. Probably connected.

And this seemed to prove whoever was behind this also had a motive.

Vengeance.

But why? Finley's company didn't exactly develop any controversial technology.

As Finley began to drift to sleep on his shoulder, Brandon gently nudged her. He'd love nothing more than to stay here and let her rest against him.

But she'd be better off lying down in bed where she could truly get a good night's rest.

"Finley," he whispered.

Her eyes fluttered open, and her sleepy gaze met his. "Yes?"

"You should get some sleep." Brandon rose and helped her to her feet then walked her to the bedroom where she'd be staying tonight.

He paused there and pressed his lips against hers. More than anything, he wished he could crawl into bed beside her.

That's the way it should be right now.

He didn't want to dwell too much on what could have been. What should have been.

As a SEAL, he'd been taught to keep focused on the road ahead.

But his disappointment felt palpable, like a physical ache in his heart.

Brandon prayed tomorrow would be a better day, one full of answers . . . and maybe even resolution.

CHAPTER
NINE

DESPITE HER EXHAUSTION, Finley couldn't sleep.

She tried for a long time until she finally threw the covers off and rose.

She walked toward the window and peered out.

It was so dark and quiet out here at the secluded mountain estate.

If circumstances were different, she might even enjoy this place.

Looking back will only make you fall forward.

Her dad's words slammed into her mind.

Finley needed to remember that truth. But she desperately prayed that today might hold some answers. The sooner she could put an end to these nasty accusations, the better.

She sucked in a breath when she saw something

move near the edge of the property where the tree line rose.

Was that a shadow of a person?

She squinted and stepped back from the window just in case anyone was watching.

She knew Blackout operatives were stationed around the property.

Was that who she'd seen?

Or had one of her enemies followed her here? Maybe even the person who'd set her up?

Cold fear seemed to pierce into her soul.

She watched but saw no more movement.

She blinked. She must have been seeing things. Her mind was playing tricks on her.

No one should know she was here.

She stared another moment. When she saw nothing, she slunk back from the window and closed the curtains.

There was no need to tell Brandon. She already knew he had his guys monitoring the place. What she'd seen was probably just the shadows of tree branches swaying in the breeze.

She was on edge.

She sank onto the bed and frowned.

If Finley were honest with herself, she knew it was only a matter of time before the person behind this found her.

Or maybe that wasn't what her enemy wanted at

all. Maybe the person behind this simply wanted to see her destroyed.

Once people realized Brandon was affiliated with her, how would that affect him? What if he was fired from his job? Or if people began to threaten him? How could Finley live with herself if all of this somehow ended up hurting the man she loved?

She already knew the answer to that question.

She couldn't.

Heaviness pressed in on her as she continued to consider the implications.

————

With Finley tucked safely in her room, Brandon headed back downstairs. There was no way he could rest.

Not until he knew more information.

Dylan and Maddox appeared and nodded toward the door.

"We're just about to take a walk outside," Dylan started. "Want to come?"

"You notice trouble out there?" Brandon asked, anticipating worst-case scenarios.

"No, but I'd like to see things for myself," Maddox said. "I thought you might want to clear your head also."

"Sounds like a plan. Let's go."

They stepped out the back door, and the cool

mountain air surrounded them. It felt refreshing, and Brandon took a deep breath.

Two other Blackout agents had arrived and were patrolling out here also. Brandon wanted to take every precaution possible, given what they were up against.

"How's Finley doing?" Maddox asked as they began to walk toward the back of the property.

Brandon pictured the exhaustion in Finley's eyes. "About as well as can be expected."

"And how are you doing?" Dylan studied his gaze, his tone making it clear he really wanted to know.

Brandon ran a hand through his hair. "To be honest, I don't know. I don't think this has all sunk in yet."

"We're going to figure out who did this to Finley. We find the motive, we find the culprit." Maddox let his words hang in the air a moment.

"True. I'm anxious to dig into those suspects Finley gave us earlier. The problem is, so much of this crime was done digitally. There's really no way to check alibis because anyone could hop on their computer wherever they were to do this kind of dirty work. Maybe even use their cell phone or a tablet."

"So we look at their finances," Maddox said as they skirted around the labyrinth at the center of the backyard and headed toward the back of the property. "See if we can trace their computers. Check with the bank to see where the money came from. Talk to their friends to see just how big the chip on their shoulder is."

Brandon tilted his head. "You and I both know that's going to be easier said than done."

Dylan's jaw twitched, but he didn't deny Brandon's statement. "Finley might be your best chance at finding that information. She has her father's tech smarts as well as business sense."

"She does. But if she's caught digging into things, it could make things even worse for her."

Dylan nodded and frowned. "You're right. We're going to figure something out. In the meantime, we're going to keep her safe."

Brandon's phone beeped. He glanced at the screen and squinted.

The couple renting out his old place had texted him.

"Excuse me a minute," Brandon muttered. Then he clicked on the message.

His chest tightened as he read the words there.

"What is it?" Dylan asked.

"I'm renting out my old condo . . . the windows were just smashed, and someone painted graffiti on the wall."

"Graffiti?"

"It said 'traitor.'"

Someone had targeted him, probably as another way of making Finley pay.

This whole ordeal was far from being over, wasn't it?

As if on cue, something clattered in the brush in the distance.

Brandon drew his gun.

Was someone out there?

He couldn't be sure.

But they needed to find out.

CHAPTER
TEN

BRANDON, Maddox, and Dylan split up as they approached the woods.

Each of them had their guns drawn, just in case.

There was no way anyone should have found them here. They had been careful to cover their tracks.

Then again, they were dealing with someone intelligent and highly sophisticated. They had to consider every possibility.

As he got closer to the shrubs where he had seen the movement, his muscles tensed. He had no idea what he was going to find on the other side of them.

It might not have been anything except the wind or a wild animal.

Or it could have been something. Someone.

Although, somebody who went through all the trouble to plant evidence entirely based in the cyberworld most likely wouldn't come out here on foot to try to wreak havoc. It didn't fit their MO.

But Brandon would still check this out.

He reached the shrubs and quietly circled to the other side.

But nobody and nothing was there.

Had it been an animal that had fled?

He couldn't be sure.

Maddox and Dylan joined him a few moments later.

"Anything?" Maddox asked.

Brandon shook his head. "No. You?"

"Nothing," Dylan said.

Brandon pulled out his flashlight and shone it on the ground.

Some of the leaves there were definitely trampled. But the ground was dry, and finding any prints would be difficult.

Still, his muscles felt tight as he considered the possibility that someone had been out here watching them.

He didn't like that idea.

Not at all.

"Maybe we should get back inside," Brandon said. "Just in case."

"Good idea," Maddox said. "Let's go."

————

Finley awoke with a start.

She shot up in bed and blinked as she realized darkness surrounded her.

But not the darkness of a jail cell.

She was thankful for that.

Then she remembered that she had come to Taryn's place. That Brandon was here.

That she was safe.

But would she ever really feel safe again?

She had trouble thinking she would, especially after everything that had happened.

Cold sweat covered her skin, she realized. Why was that? Had she been having a bad dream?

It seemed as if she would remember it if that were the case.

Then she heard a squeak.

Her lungs froze.

Was someone else in this dark room with her?

She searched the shadows, looking for any signs that her instincts were correct.

But if someone was in here right now, they blended in.

She knew she should move. That she should grab her phone. Call for help.

Yet she couldn't move. Couldn't do anything.

Finally, she cleared her throat. "Who's in here?"

There was no answer.

Not that she'd really expected there to be an answer.

But the layout of her room was odd, almost an L shape. And the bathroom was to her right, the door to the hallway beyond that, almost like a hotel room.

Then she heard a soft thud.

Her heart beat in overtime.

What if somebody was in here with her?

Suddenly, she snapped out of her stupor.

She reached onto the nightstand beside her and grabbed her phone. She hit the screen so she could dial Brandon's number.

And as she did, she heard a soft click.

Was that the door?

Had there been someone in here, and had that person just left?

Quickly, she scrambled out of bed. Adrenaline propelled her forward.

She hit the flashlight on her phone and turned it on.

The corridor in front of the doorway was empty.

As she passed the bathroom, she quickly shined her light inside that open door.

It appeared empty also.

She rushed to her bedroom door and threw it open.

If someone had been in here, she wanted to know who.

But as she peered out into the hallway, she saw nobody was there.

Had that whole thing just been her imagination?

CHAPTER
ELEVEN

WHEN FINLEY AWOKE the next morning, it was past eight o'clock—late for her. She'd always been an early riser.

She sat up in bed, her white sheets falling at her waist and a chill washing over her.

At once, reality crashed back down around her. Awful, awful reality.

She'd hoped the events of the past few days were just a nightmare, but she knew better.

And what about last night?

Had someone actually been in her room?

She shivered again.

She had no proof of it. The whole thing could have been her imagination.

For that reason, she hadn't called Brandon. He needed his rest also, and Finley had a feeling her lack of sleep was causing her imagination to be overly dramatic.

With a sigh, she pulled her blanket up higher around her neck, wishing she could stay in bed forever.

But she couldn't.

She desperately wanted to hope that today would hold better news, but she had to face the reality of this situation. Better news might not ever happen.

She grabbed her phone again and checked for any updates on the case. She knew it probably wasn't wise to search the internet. She *definitely* knew she shouldn't read the things people were writing about her online.

But how could she not? She needed to make informed decisions. Making informed decisions required knowing the facts. It wasn't as if the FBI would offer her information about her own case.

She searched her name, and pages and pages of articles appeared. Pages of articles about what she had done. Profiles of her. Profiles of her father. Information on reportedly how much money she had received from this deal.

Even though she hadn't received any money—not by her own volition.

Then she looked up information on the scene outside Embolden's office yesterday.

Two people had been arrested for setting off that

bomb. The explosion hadn't hurt anyone. It had simply been done to send a message.

Which was no doubt what someone had wanted.

What else did these people have in store as they tried to teach her a lesson? It was a double whammy. Not only was Finley facing federal charges, but now an angry mob was after her because of what she'd supposedly done.

With a frown, she put her phone down and closed her eyes.

It was time to face reality.

She would put on some clean clothes and get ready for the day. At least, she'd be able to see Brandon. He was the one bright spot in all this.

However, she should have woken up beside him this morning.

With him as her husband and her as his wife.

She ran her hand across the sheets beside her, mourning what she'd lost.

She shoved those thoughts aside. She was spending too much time feeling sorry for herself and not enough time searching for solutions.

For now, she needed to see what today held.

Last night, Brandon had told her his guys would look into the suspects she'd mentioned. It was probably too early for them to have discovered anything. But she hoped and prayed that would be the short-term outcome.

Maybe sometime today they could narrow down the list.

But as soon as she stepped out of the shower and pulled her clothes on, someone urgently knocked on her door. "Finley? Are you up?"

Brandon.

She rushed to the door and threw it open.

When Finley saw the concern on his face, she knew something was wrong.

Her stomach roiled.

What now?

———

"Somehow, this address was just leaked to the public," Brandon explained to Finley as she stood in front of him with her hair coming down in wet tendrils around her face.

Finley's eyebrows flung upward as she gasped. "What?"

He nodded, hating the fact he had to break this news to her. "You need to grab your things, and we need to get out of here before anyone shows up. The gates should hold people back, but we can't take any chances right now—not given everything that's happened."

Her mind raced. "How in the world was the address leaked?"

"We'll figure that out later. For now, grab your

things. There's a back way off the property. We need to go. Now."

Brandon watched as Finley quickly stuffed things into her suitcase. He hated to do this to her. Hated to uproot her again from what should have been a safe place.

But they had no other choice right now. Her safety was his first priority.

After stuffing everything back into the suitcase, she returned to him.

He wasn't used to seeing his fiancée looking so vulnerable. She was so smart and such a strong, confident leader.

But the events of the past few days had shaken her to the core, and Brandon couldn't blame her for that. There was no time for her to even dry her hair or do her makeup right now.

They had to leave.

"Do you have everything?" He took the bag from her.

"I do." Finley nodded, but her eyes looked dazed. Exhaustion etched itself into the lines on her forehead, into the dullness of her skin.

Before Brandon left the room, he leaned forward and brushed his lips across her cheek. Then he pulled her into a quick hug and murmured, "It's going to be okay."

Those words were all he could give her right now.

He didn't know what okay looked like. He didn't know what okay meant.

He only knew they would get through this together, no matter the outcome.

The almost blank expression remained in Finley's eyes as she murmured, "Thank you."

Brandon took her hand and led her down the hallway. The rest of the crew was already waiting in two SUVs at the back of the property.

Maddox was behind the wheel again, Dylan at his side, and Amanda was seated in the back. Brandon put the bag in the trunk area then climbed in beside Finley.

He double tapped the seat in front of him with his palm. "Let's go."

Maddox took off. "Two cars have already pulled up out front. It's only a matter of time before others arrive."

Brandon knew his colleague's words were true. People would start showing up en masse soon.

Maddox started toward the back of the property to an old service road that cut through the mountains there. He knew this place better than the rest of them since he'd spent the most time here with Taryn.

Brandon was trying to figure out where they should go next, where Finley might be safe.

But really, he wished to simply be on his honeymoon, relaxing and enjoying time with his wife.

He couldn't think about what could have been. He had to focus on the now.

Just as that thought went through his mind, a gunshot filled the air.

The back glass shattered.

"Get down!" He put his arm around Finley and pushed her below the seat as adrenaline surged through him.

Amanda screamed and ducked also.

Someone had been hiding in the woods, just waiting for the opportunity to shoot at them.

His heart raced.

That person had just taken this to the next level.

CHAPTER
TWELVE

FINLEY'S HEARTBEAT kicked up another notch.

Someone was shooting at them?

Was this another person bent on revenge because they thought she was responsible for the death of those soldiers?

What she wouldn't do to have those Rangers back. But she had nothing to do with their deaths. She would never purposefully put other people in danger. She wasn't greedy and gladly gave her money away to those in need. Her purpose in life wasn't to be wealthy.

Another bullet sounded.

Maddox swerved.

The SUV rumbled.

She felt them tilt.

Then Maddox righted the vehicle. He hit the

accelerator and sped down the gravel road—and away from the shooter.

They left that gunman behind—but she worried there could be more waiting for them.

Dylan was already on the phone reporting the incident. Law enforcement would need to investigate. But this wasn't the time for Brandon and his crew to stop.

Brandon didn't have to tell her that. Finley already knew.

They wove through several back mountain roads, silence filling the car until they hit a highway.

Finley didn't bother to ask where they were going. It didn't matter. Because she didn't have any great ideas about where she should hide out.

Finally, Amanda spoke, her face pale and voice somber. "I hate to say it, but this is going to dominate every headline and TV news special for a long time. You need to be prepared for the storm you're facing right now."

Finley nodded. "I know."

Amanda frowned and stared out the window.

"You're getting threats too, aren't you?" Finley studied her friend.

"Don't worry about me." She waved a hand in the air to brush off her statement.

"But you *are* getting threats." Apprehension thrummed through Finley at the realization.

Amanda's gaze connected with her. "I'll be fine."

"Amanda . . ."

Her friend squeezed her arm reassuringly. "I'm a big girl, and I make my own decisions. You're my friend, and I'm going to help you out. I know you didn't do this."

"How did they find our location?" Finley decided to focus on something else at the moment rather than wallowing in her regret.

"Let me see your phone." Brandon extended his hand toward her.

"My phone isn't traceable," she reminded him again. "My company developed this tech."

"But if someone at Embolden is in on this, then maybe they know some kind of backdoor access that cuts off the security of your program."

Finley's stomach clenched. She didn't like the thought of that, but he had a good point.

She handed him her phone. The next moment, Brandon lowered his window and tossed it out onto the side of the road.

"If they were tracking us that way, they're not anymore," he muttered.

Finley wanted to argue. But at least all her information, data, and photos were stored on the Cloud.

There was no time to waste if they wanted to get out of here. They couldn't risk being followed again.

But was there anywhere Finley would truly be safe?

———

After much thought and consideration, Brandon arranged for everyone to head back to Lantern Beach. A helicopter was due to arrive at a small airport about an hour away from the estate where they'd been staying.

So far, no one appeared to have followed them to this location. Currently, no one else was in the lobby. If anyone did show up, Brandon had arranged for his group to use one of the offices here so they could maintain their privacy.

"How in the world was the address leaked?" Finley paced as they waited inside the small lobby.

Her hair had dried in waves, and her face was still makeup free.

Brandon loved the natural look on her.

But this wasn't the time to dwell on how beautiful Finley was or how thankful he was to have her in his life.

Brandon paused near the front door, remaining close—just in case. "The only thing that makes sense is that someone was tracking your phone."

"But if someone was tracking my phone, that means they had access to my information that's on the phone." Finley absently began to play with the ends of her hair, twirling various strands as she paced.

"Which again proves that whoever is behind this

is brilliant," Amanda added. She sat stiffly in a chair, her purse on her lap and a pensive expression on her face.

"Then once they had my location, what did they do?" Finley continued. "Tell the mobs so they could follow me?"

"Maybe someone wants the angry masses to make you pay, just in case the justice system fails." Amanda shrugged.

Brandon didn't like the sound of that. But Amanda was telling the truth. It was a distinct possibility.

Dylan strode toward them, his phone in his hand. "I just got an update on Ryan Hold."

Finley stopped pacing. "And?"

"It turns out he just had surgery last week."

"Surgery?" Finley repeated. "For what?"

"A brain tumor."

Her eyebrows flew up. "I guess that would explain his off-the-wall behavior. Does this mean he's not guilty?"

"That's what I'd guess," Brandon said. "I mean, I suppose he could have orchestrated this before his surgery, and it's playing out now. But I find that unlikely."

Dylan frowned, looking as if he had more to say.

"What is it?" Brandon asked.

"I sent Titus to talk to him," Dylan said. "When

he heard what happened to Finley, Titus said Ryan almost looked happy about it."

Finley let out a long breath. "I can't say it surprises me. But Ryan's not in his right mind currently."

"We'll look into Talen and Victor as well," Brandon assured her. "In fact, I'd like to talk to Talen face-to-face myself. He's been developing some AI technology, and the man is clearly smart."

"I could go too . . ." Finley stared at him, waiting for his reaction.

"I think it's better if you stay secluded. Every time you go out, you're a target."

She clamped her mouth shut and didn't argue.

His words were true.

She was going to need to watch her every step.

———

Finley finally gave up pacing and sat down beside Amanda.

The two of them had been friends for more than a decade. They'd met at the private school they both attended, but Amanda hadn't been like some of the other girls there. She'd been friendly and down-to-earth.

The two had hit it off right away and had stayed in touch over the years. Though they only saw each other once or twice a year, their bond was strong.

"You holding up okay?" Amanda turned to observe her, a cup of vending machine coffee in her hands.

Finley nodded. "I guess so. I just can't believe all of this."

"I can't either. I can't imagine what kind of person would want to do this to you."

"Me either." Finley frowned as she stared at Brandon, who talked to his colleagues near the door.

The helicopter should be here any moment.

"Finley . . . I have a confession to make." Amanda pressed her lips together.

"What's wrong?" She braced herself for whatever her friend had to say.

"A reporter—some guy named John Clark—called me yesterday evening after I went to bed. I usually only answer numbers I recognize, but I was sleepy. I thought it was someone from the office. I didn't talk long, nor did I tell this guy anything. But I wonder . . . I wonder if I was on the line long enough that he traced the call. I'm so sorry, Finley. What if this is my fault?"

Finley squeezed her hand. "Don't think like that. Even if that is the way someone found out my location, you couldn't have known."

Amanda shook her head. "I can't even stomach the thought of it."

"Most likely, it was *my* phone they traced. Somehow, we just need to get ahead of the person who's behind this, but right now that feels impossible."

"I agree. Eventually, we're probably going to need to do a press conference or something to try to stay ahead of this. But I just don't think it's time yet."

"I agree. We need to let this shake out more first. How are you holding up?" Finley decided the medicine for her self-pity was to turn the attention onto someone else.

Only three months ago, Amanda had lost her husband of six years. He'd taken his own life.

"I'm hanging in. It's been difficult." Amanda swallowed hard as if fighting emotions.

Finley squeezed her friend's arm, hating that Amanda had to go through this horrific tragedy. "I can only imagine. I'm so sorry."

Finley had even been worried about asking her to be a part of the wedding after everything that had happened. But Amanda had insisted she'd be okay, that she wanted to be here. Finley had no choice but to take her friend's word for it.

Friendships with other women were hard to come by for Finley. Not only did she work a lot, which made it hard to cultivate friendships, but not long ago an old friend had betrayed her—all in an effort to get rich herself.

Finley was still learning to trust again. Thankfully, she'd quickly bonded with the girlfriends of many of Brandon's friends.

"I only wished Jerry had talked to me first . . ." Amanda stared off into the distance. "I had no idea he was contemplating taking his own life. If I'd known . . ."

"He seemed so happy and normal the last time I saw him." That had been two weeks before his suicide. "It still baffles me also. And now you've been left with questions that he took to the grave with him. I'm so sorry about that."

Amanda's frown deepened. "I thought things were going great. But I found out while talking to our financial advisor that Jerry made a bad investment—and he was paranoid that it would ruin us. We could have moved past that. I just wish he would have realized that."

Finley glanced at Brandon again. She was so thankful to still have him.

Unfortunately, other people's losses often reminded her of what she could also lose. She didn't ever want to take the people in her life for granted.

"Oh, no." Amanda sat up straighter as she stared at her phone. "This isn't good."

"What's not good?" Finley shifted closer.

Amanda showed Finley her phone screen.

It was a photo of Finley talking with a member of China's NPC—National People's Congress. Muchen Weng.

"That's not me," Finley muttered, her head swirling. "I've never met that man."

"It must be a deep fake," Amanda said. "But it looks real. And people with social media . . . you know how they are. They will believe anything they see sometimes."

"I'm guilty before proven innocent, aren't I? I don't know how I'm going to win this." She pressed her eyes closed.

"Does Embolden have the technology to create something like this?"

Finley heard Amanda's question, but it barely registered as her head spun.

CHAPTER
THIRTEEN

FOUR HOURS LATER, Finley and Brandon approached Lantern Beach via helicopter. Below her, she could see the ocean along with the sandy barrier island she hoped to call home one day.

She saw the Ferris wheel, the boardwalk, even the church where she and Brandon should have been married.

Then she spotted Blackout Headquarters—and the crowd gathered at the gate surrounding it.

Her heart lurched into her throat.

There was nowhere she could go to escape this, was there? This would be her life for the considerable future.

She frowned at the thought and crossed her arms as she waited to land.

Amanda had decided to head back to her office in

Fayetteville and work on things from there. She wanted to have her colleagues help her, and being confined in Lantern Beach would hinder the work she needed to do. Titus would stay with her and would act as security.

Finley liked staying at the Daniel Oliver Building, where she had an apartment already. She came nearly every weekend to visit Brandon.

She felt safe there. And welcome.

Finley stared at the crowd near the gate as her thoughts drifted.

She just needed one lead in order to move forward.

Brandon had mentioned earlier that he would drop her off here and then head up to Norfolk to visit Talen.

Since Talen's new company worked on AI, he was their best lead. Brandon said he wanted to look the man in the eye as they spoke. Wanted to see his facial expressions. Meanwhile, she'd promised to stay here, where it was safer.

She glanced beside her as something caught her eye.

She sucked in a breath.

Was that a . . . drone?

Brandon seemed to see it at the same time she did.

He leaned forward and twisted around, speaking into his headset as he talked to the pilot.

His urgent actions put her on edge.

A drone?

What was someone trying to do? Take footage of her landing here?

It seemed the most likely scenario.

But the next instant, Brandon shouted a warning.

She heard metal on metal.

The helicopter lurched.

The drone had run into the blades, hadn't it?

Then her stomach nearly flew from her body as the helicopter began to freefall.

———

Brandon grasped Finley's hand as he felt the copter falling.

That drone had hit the blades. Knocked them out of operation.

He was thankful they'd already begun their descent and had been only thirty feet from landing.

But thirty feet was enough to do a lot of damage.

"Brace yourself," he muttered into his headset.

He glanced at Finley and saw her close her eyes.

In the front, the pilot struggled to gain control.

There was still a possibility they could land this thing without a crash. He'd seen it happen before as a Navy SEAL.

But that would take extreme skill from the pilot.

He prayed a safe landing would be the outcome now also.

"Hold on tight!" the helicopter pilot shouted.

The next moment, Brandon felt a jarring bounce. He released Finley's hand and braced himself.

Another jolting impact hit them.

He lurched forward.

After one more bounce, the helicopter landed.

They were safe.

But his relief was short-lived.

A smoky scent filled his nostrils.

They needed to get out of here.

He undid his seatbelt and then Finley's. He grabbed her hand with one hand as he opened the door with the other. "We need to get away from this. Now."

He glanced at the pilot as well as Maddox and the rest of the crew.

Everyone appeared uninjured as they evacuated the copter.

Just as they reached the sidewalk leading to the Daniel Oliver Building, a blast filled the air.

Brandon shielded Finley from the explosion.

When it was safe, he couldn't help but look back.

That had been close.

Too close.

If they'd been in that copter just a couple minutes longer, none of them would be here right now.

Finley buried herself in his chest as sirens filled the air in the distance.

Danger appeared to be hitting them from every side.

And this was far from being over.

CHAPTER
FOURTEEN

FINLEY WATCHED as firefighters put out the flames.

She couldn't believe that had happened.

The police were there, questioning people. She had heard a rumor that a reporter was being arrested for flying the drone.

John Clark.

The same reporter who'd called Amanda.

From the sounds of it, the rookie reporter hadn't meant any harm. He'd simply wanted to get video footage for the news station he worked for in hopes of being promoted.

And it had almost resulted in innocent people losing their lives.

The police were questioning him, but he claimed he hadn't made that phone call to Amanda. He also said he hadn't leaked their location.

But there was more to it than that.

Finley had also seen Brandon and Colton talking together.

Something else was wrong, wasn't it?

But Finley hadn't had a chance to ask Brandon what they'd been talking about.

Not until Brandon walked with her to her room.

Once Finley and Brandon were alone, she peered out the window and took a deep breath. "What's going on, Brandon?"

The flames were out now. The reporter had been taken away.

But the crowd remained. Still protesting.

Even through all that had happened.

The people still wanted blood, didn't they?

Brandon shrugged as he paced near the window. "It's nothing you need to worry about."

She placed a hand on his arm, realizing he was trying to protect her. But she needed to know. "Whatever it is, I can handle it."

He pressed his lips together in a frown and briefly looked away before his eyes met hers again. "People are calling for a boycott on Blackout. We're working with you, which means they assume we are working with China also."

She gasped, and her hand covered her mouth. "Oh, Brandon . . . I can't let this happen to you guys. I know how these people work. They're going to look for any information they can dig up on anyone who works for Blackout, and they're going to try to use that to do an exposé on you guys and ruin your reputation."

"This will pass." He sounded confident as he said the words.

"But what damage will be done until then? Things like this can destroy people and companies. And you guys are innocent in all of this."

"So are you."

Finley pinched the skin between her eyes. "There's no need for Blackout to be destroyed."

"And what about your company?"

"I have people who are depending on me for their jobs. Maybe now that I've been temporarily suspended from my position at Embolden, the company can be salvaged, though I'm not really sure at this point. And Blackout . . . you have a lot of people depending on you also. I don't want to be the cause of the downfall."

"Why don't you let us worry about that?"

Finley frowned, unsure she'd be able to let go of her apprehension that easily.

"Hey." Brandon tugged her closer. "Don't do anything rash, okay?"

"What do you mean?"

"I mean, I don't know what is going on inside that head of yours. But you just need to give this some more time." He stroked his hand through her hair.

"You keep saying that. But the more time that passes, the worse this seems to get."

Instead of saying anything, Brandon pulled her into his arms for a long hug.

Finley leaned against him, relishing his embrace.

But she wasn't going to let more innocent people go down because of her.

She wasn't sure what that would look like. But she needed to start thinking about it long and hard. She needed to figure out a plan. Now.

Too much was at stake to leave anything to chance.

———

Thirty minutes later, Brandon left with Rocco to go talk to Talen Schultz in Norfolk.

It had seemed the helicopter exploding only brought out more crowds. The people outside the gate had to be controlled by even more Blackout agents. As he listened to the mob yelling and chanting, the apprehension in his gut grew stronger and stronger.

He had to keep Finley safe. The only way to do that was to keep her tucked away.

The problem was that Finley wasn't the type to hide away in silence. She was a fighter . . . and that could make her more of a target.

He had to find some answers and finish this.

Then he and Finley could get married. Could start the rest of their lives together.

He couldn't wait for that to happen.

Once they were past the gate, the crowds thinned, and he let out a breath.

"It's ugly out here," Rocco said, his British accent deep and rolling.

"You can say that again." Brandon rubbed his jaw as they started the long journey up to Norfolk.

They had to take the ferry to Ocracoke and then take another ferry from Ocracoke to Hatteras Island. Then they'd drive up Hatteras and over the Oregon Inlet bridge through Nags Head, Kill Devil Hills, and Kitty Hawk. They'd head to Virginia from there.

Part of him had wanted to stay with Finley. Maybe that was what he *should* be doing. He wasn't sure. He only knew he had to do *something*.

The good news was that Cassidy had promised to stop by Blackout and check on Finley. He knew Finley admired the police chief. He hoped the visit would be a good distraction and would keep Finley's thoughts occupied.

And he *really* hoped Finley wasn't considering taking matters into her own hands.

She was selfless enough that she'd want to spare him from the pain this was causing.

He couldn't let her do that.

He only knew he needed to find answers. Even though he trusted his colleagues and knew they were capable, there were some conversations he wanted to have himself.

This was one of them.

He prayed this trip wasn't a waste of time.

In fact, he'd make sure it wasn't.

CHAPTER
FIFTEEN

FINLEY CURLED ON THE COUCH, her new phone in her hands. One that wasn't registered to her. Colton had brought it up several minutes ago.

No one should be able to track her on this phone —not that it was a secret where she was located. No doubt the protesters outside the Blackout Headquarters had seen her and spread the word she was here.

That Blackout was keeping a traitor safe.

Finley frowned at the thought.

Even if she were proven innocent, would people ever truly forget? Or would this false accusation always stain her reputation?

She pressed her head back into the couch.

Her accommodations here were comfortable. The apartment was efficient with a small kitchen and living room area, a single bedroom and bathroom, and a patio big enough for two folding chairs.

Probably the worst thing she could do right now was to sit here doing nothing. She'd keep thinking in worst-case scenarios if she didn't keep her mind occupied.

She'd really wanted to go with Brandon, but she knew by the look in his eyes that he didn't think it was a good idea.

So she'd obliged.

Now she wished she hadn't. She hadn't even told her other friends here that she was back—but it didn't really matter. Most of them came on weekends, and probably weren't here right now.

A knock sounded at her door, and for a moment Finley was tempted not to answer.

Then she heard, "Finley, it's me Cassidy."

Finley sat up straighter. The police chief was here to see her? Did she have more bad news?

Finley had talked to Cassidy many times. Gone to cookouts with her and her husband, Ty. They'd attended church together.

The two had never exactly gotten together on a one-on-one basis or shared anything deep or personal.

Even so, the woman almost felt like a friend.

Finley walked to the door and opened it. Cassidy stood there with a bag in her hands, alluring scents drifting from it. "Brandon asked me to bring you some dinner."

"He shouldn't have done that." Even as Finley

said the words, the appetizing aroma of freshly baked bread and fried potatoes rose up to her.

"He said it's your favorite." Cassidy held the bag higher. "A California club with fries."

"That is my favorite. Thank you." Finley stepped back and extended her arm. "Would you like to come in?"

"I don't want to impose."

"It's fine. I need a distraction."

"In that case . . . I thought maybe you could use someone else to talk to, maybe to get a fresh perspective."

"That sounds nice."

Cassidy had a lot of experience and wisdom, and Finley would take whatever help she could get right now. Maybe Cassidy would have some insight on this that Finley hadn't yet considered.

If nothing else, a listening ear could be a blessing.

They sat at a small table beside the kitchenette, and Finley pulled out the food. Even though she wasn't that hungry, she knew she needed to eat. This *was* her favorite meal, so she hoped she might find it satisfying.

"Would you like some?" Finley nodded to her fries.

Cassidy shook her head. "I'm not hungry. Thank you."

Finley nibbled on a fry, letting its salty goodness wash over her tastebuds.

Cassidy leaned back in her chair after letting Finley eat for a couple of minutes. "Those crowds outside are crazy, aren't they?"

"They're insane. I'm sorry if they're putting more pressure on the police department."

"Don't you worry about that. It's our job."

"It still has to be a strain on things. I know you don't have a large department to start with."

"I promise you that we'll be okay," Cassidy assured her. She shifted in her seat. "Agent Bills stopped by earlier, by the way. I wasn't here, but Colton told me about it."

Finley's breath caught. "He came by here? Why?"

"He said he was checking in." Cassidy paused and pressed her lips together. "And that he wanted to remind you that he's keeping an eye on you. One slipup . . ."

"And I'm back behind bars." Finley frowned at the thought.

The feds were looking for an excuse to put her away. That's how certain they were about her guilt.

"Just follow the terms of your bail, and you'll be fine," Cassidy said. "Aside from that, I understand there are no really good leads on this case right now."

"That's right. We don't have much to work with." Finley swallowed hard, the food in her stomach feeling more like rocks. "I just want to figure out this guy's motive. Then I'll feel like I can track him down."

Cassidy nodded slowly as if in thought. "I have a hard time thinking anyone would hate you on a personal level like this."

"I didn't think I had that many enemies. At least, not before all this happened. But there are plenty of reasons for people to hate me and my company."

Cassidy shifted, leaning with one elbow on the table. "Are there any particular clients or groups of people who'd have a reason to do this to you? Other than this accusation that's out there that you sold secrets."

Finley let out a breath and lowered the fry in her hands. "That's what I keep thinking about. I have a list of all our recent clients, and I've been reviewing them, but nothing has really rung a bell."

"That's too bad. That would be a good place to start."

Finley's phone buzzed.

Was it Brandon? As far as she knew, only a few people had this new number.

But when she glanced at her screen, Finley saw it wasn't Brandon.

It was a text message from a number she didn't recognize.

Are you suffering enough yet? I don't think so.

The blood drained from her face.

This person had her new phone number.

But how? No one had it.

No one but Brandon, Amanda, and Colton.

Just as quickly as the message had appeared, it was gone.

That meant Finley couldn't prove that the message had ever been sent.

If she'd been thinking more quickly, she would have taken a screenshot. But she hadn't thought of that, and now it was too late.

Even if she told the feds, she doubted they'd believe her.

That was probably just what this person wanted.

To completely destroy her.

But why?

———

After a very long drive, Brandon and Rocco finally arrived at the office building where Talen Schultz had set up his company. The two of them had killed time on the drive by chatting about Finley's charges. Brandon had also made some phone calls.

Talen's office was located in downtown Norfolk in one of the high rises along the Elizabeth River.

It was already 3:30, so Brandon hoped he was still there.

The parking garage was full, and Rocco had to

find a space on the top floor of a five-story garage.

Several minutes later, they were inside the building and headed toward the eighth floor.

Talen's new company was called Smart Intelligence, and it appeared to take up the entire floor.

A middle-aged receptionist eyed them as they stepped inside. "Can I help you?"

"We need to talk to Mr. Schultz, please," Brandon started.

Her expression remained professional. "Do you have an appointment?"

"No," Brandon said. "We don't. But it's about a rather important matter."

"I'm afraid he doesn't see anybody without an appointment."

"We've driven a long way to talk to him." Brandon had known this could be a possibility, but he hoped that things would work out. He'd tried to set up something beforehand, but he hadn't been granted a time slot.

"I'm sorry," the receptionist said. "But I can't help you. I don't make his schedule. I just enforce it." She offered a tight smile.

"Can you tell us if he's here in the office?" Rocco asked.

Her gaze wavered back and forth between the two of them as if she weren't sure if she should answer or not. Finally, she said, "Yes, he's here."

"Could you just ask him if he'd be able to talk to

us?" Brandon shifted, hoping there was a way he could get through to him. "We're old friends of Jim Cooper. It's about an urgent matter."

She eyed them skeptically one more time before sighing. "I'll see what I can do."

A surge of hope rushed through him, and he prayed this trip wouldn't be in vain.

She murmured a few things into the phone before turning to them. "I'm sorry, but he's not available."

Brandon didn't want to give up so easily, but he couldn't just barge in there either. His gaze caught Rocco's for a moment.

Rocco gave him a slight nod as if encouraging him not to give up.

"Tell him it's concerning Finley Cooper," Brandon added.

The woman hesitated.

"Please."

She shook her head but picked up the phone again. A moment later she looked up. "He said he could give you five minutes."

Brandon smiled. "That's perfect."

Moments after he said the words, the door near the receptionist opened.

Talen Schultz stepped out, and he didn't exactly look happy to see them.

The man, who was probably in his mid-sixties with thinning salt-and-pepper hair, had a button nose and slightly hunched shoulders.

But it was the beady look in his eyes that really caught Brandon's attention.

He instantly did not trust this guy.

"Come to my office," he said without so much as an introduction.

Brandon and Rocco glanced at each other, exchanging a silent conversation, before following the man down the hallway to an oversized office at the back of the building.

As soon as they were inside, he shut the door in a crisp motion and then pointed to two leather chairs. "Sit."

This would be a fun conversation, Brandon mused. He could already tell.

"You're friends with Finley?" He glanced back and forth between the two of them as he sat behind his massive desk.

"I'm her fiancé," Brandon stated. "And this is one of my colleagues."

Talen stared at him, curiosity lighting his gaze. "I see. I'm sorry to hear about what happened to her, though I can't say I'm surprised. How can I help you?"

He couldn't say he was surprised? Brandon tensed. What did that even mean?

"Wait . . ." Brandon tilted his head. "Why are you not surprised?"

"Well, if Finley's anything like her father, then her main goal is to make as much money as possible."

Brandon had met Finley's dad, and he hadn't gotten that impression from the man.

"Is that why you guys parted company?" Rocco asked.

Brandon knew what Finley had told him—that the two men's visions for the company had been different. Brandon was interested to hear what Talen would say.

"That's right. He wanted to go where we could make the most money." A touch of bitterness flickered in his gaze. "That was more important to him than innovation and creating new tech. In the end, I've got to say that it was a good thing we went our separate ways."

Brandon glanced around the office where no expense had been spared. "You're doing pretty well for yourself then?"

A flicker of pride lit Talen's gaze. "That's right. We're doing great things here at Smart Intelligence."

"Including some work with artificial intelligence, as I understand." Brandon stared at the man, not wanting to miss any spark of deceit that might flash in the man's gaze.

"Yes, that is part of our focus." He jutted his chin up. "I didn't need Jim Cooper to succeed. I'm doing just fine on my own."

But there was something about the man's underlying tone that made Brandon wonder if that was truly the case or not.

CHAPTER
SIXTEEN

"WHAT IS IT?" Cassidy leaned closer as Finley stared at her phone.

Finley explained the disappearing messages, still in disbelief herself.

Cassidy pulled her gaze away from the phone. "Who has access to that kind of tech?"

Finley frowned. "I wish I knew. No one at Embolden."

"Are you sure?" Cassidy studied her face as if hoping Finley had simply forgotten about something.

But Finley's answer was unwavering. "My team runs everything past me first. I'd know about technology like this."

Cassidy leaned back and her jaw tightened as she seemed to think everything through. "Everything is complicated when so many crimes can take place by someone sitting behind the keyboard. That fact makes it harder to catch the culprit sometimes. You probably have technology that will capture people's every keystroke, right?"

"We do. In fact, we have that technology on the computers at work. I would imagine that the person behind this is too smart to do this at their workstation."

"But it is possible, correct?"

At those words, her thoughts began to percolate.

Could this be from someone inside Embolden?

She didn't have access to her company's server anymore.

But . . .

Her thoughts rushed ahead of her.

"One more question . . ." Cassidy shifted. "Where were you when this supposed deal with China went down?"

Finley nibbled the inside of her lip a moment. "It had to have happened shortly before those Rangers were killed, which would have placed it in mid-May I suppose."

"This might be a wild goose chase, but were you doing anything in particular during that time? Anything that could give you an alibi?"

Finley's thoughts raced through her schedule during that month, and she sat up straighter. "You're right. Why didn't I think of that?"

Cassidy squinted. "Think of what?"

"The timeline! And why didn't the FBI ask me

that? Is it because their minds were simply made up already?"

"I suppose they could have thought that cash payment was what they needed to seal their case. What are you thinking?"

"I went down to Ecuador on a two-week mission trip with some other people from my church in Raleigh."

Cassidy's eyes lit with excitement. "Did you have internet access while you were there?"

"No, I was unplugged. I didn't even bring my laptop with me. But I did share a small room with three other women. They could tell the FBI I was there."

"That just might be the piece of evidence you need to prove you couldn't be behind this."

Finley nodded quickly. "I'm going to have to narrow down the time when they think this happened. Maybe Amanda can let me know that for sure. But if it did happen when I was in Ecuador then . . . maybe I don't need to find the person who's guilty. Maybe I just need to prove that I'm innocent."

Finley felt another surge of hope.

Maybe—just maybe—she wouldn't spend the rest of her life in prison.

"What exactly are you here for?" Talen leveled his gaze at them.

Brandon shifted in the leather seat. "We're trying to figure out who might not like Finley or her father enough to set her up."

He raised his eyebrows. "Set her up?"

"She's not guilty of these crimes," Brandon stated, his voice unwavering.

A touch of smugness—and doubt—filled his gaze. "You seem very confident of that."

"I am." Brandon stared at the man. "I'm confident enough in that assessment that I'm not afraid to ask you if you might be the one who's behind this."

The man's eyebrows flew up. "Me? Why would I do something like that?"

"I heard there was bad blood between you and Mr. Cooper."

"That's all water under the bridge." Talen waved his hand in the air to brush Brandon off.

"So you admit you two had issues?"

"Anyone in business together has disagreements."

"The kind that leads toward vengeance?" Brandon pulled a picture from his pocket and slid it across the desk toward Talen. "What does this look like to you?"

Talen stared at the picture and his eyes widened. "This looks like evidence to prove that she's guilty."

"It's a fake," Brandon said.

Talen didn't look surprised by his statement. "Technology is an amazing and terrifying thing at times, isn't it?"

"I know your company develops technology that can create photos like this."

Talen bristled. "So you think that I'm responsible for this photo?"

Brandon didn't say anything. Instead, he just waited for the man to continue.

"I didn't do this. I have more important things to do than to ruminate on the past and how I may or may not have been wronged."

"If you're not behind this, then who do you think is?"

"Have you looked into Victor Newman?"

"Victor Newman?" That was the man Finley had gone on a couple of dates with. "Why would you suspect him?"

"Because he contacted me a few weeks ago . . . he showed up here at my office. Much like the two of you did." He paused as if to drive home his point. "He was asking about Finley. And he had a strange look in his eyes."

CHAPTER SEVENTEEN

"WHAT DO you think of that guy?" Brandon asked as he and Rocco left.

After exactly five minutes, Talen had stood and pointed to the door.

Brandon and Rocco had reluctantly departed.

"I'm not sure if I think he's the best suspect yet or if we should look into Victor Newman," Brandon muttered as they stepped into the elevator. "Maybe a little bit of both."

"Agreed. If what Talen said is true, then Victor's timing was suspicious. But there's something I didn't like about that Talen guy. I'm not saying he set Finley up for treason. But I definitely wouldn't want to work with him."

"You can say that again." Brandon flipped the keys in his hands as they stepped into the parking garage. They took the stairs to the fifth floor, and

Brandon noticed that there were a few more empty parking spaces nearby.

He hit the button on the SUV's remote, and the vehicle let out three small beeps.

Then he and Rocco climbed inside to begin the trip back to Lantern Beach.

Really, this was too much to do in a day. The trip home would take at least four hours.

But Brandon had wanted to see Talen with his own eyes.

After he started the SUV, he sat there for a moment. "Is there anything else we need to do while we're in Norfolk?"

"Not as far as I'm concerned. But I'm open to whatever you might be considering." Rocco shrugged.

Brandon shook his head. "I'm not sure right now."

Just as he started to put the SUV into Reverse, he heard another car speeding through the parking garage, going entirely too fast.

A dark green sports car whipped around the corner, tires squealing.

He waited for the vehicle to pass.

But as he waited, the Charger came straight at them.

He didn't even have time to warn Rocco before the vehicle rammed into them at full speed.

Brandon's SUV jerked forward, plowed through the guardrail, and dangled above the street below.

———

Cassidy only stayed for a few more minutes until Finley finished eating. Then she said she needed to get home for the evening.

Finley thanked her for stopping by and for the food. Cassidy had been a nice distraction from her problems, and Finley truly did appreciate it.

But her thoughts were still racing.

Not only had Cassidy given her a lot to think about, but her mind kept wandering in different directions—from ways she might be able to access the computers to some of the people she suspected could be behind this.

The FBI weren't looking at anybody else. So the person behind this must have the capability of destroying any type of information trail that could be out there.

But everything left a footprint. Everything.

And Finley had just enough computer skills that she might be able to find those footprints—but she needed to access a computer and the internet first.

As part of her company's policy, everything their employees did on their work computers was monitored. Embolden had a program for that. And the program was installed from simply clicking on a link.

If she could somehow send an e-mail with a link her suspects could click on, that could give her backdoor access to their computers.

To do so without their knowledge or permission would be extremely illegal. Her bail might even be revoked.

But it also might be the only way Finley could find out the information she needed.

Sure, Finley might have an alibi, and she truly hoped that worked in her favor. But she feared the FBI might still think she was behind these acts, that they'd think she'd manipulated any tracking recorded on her devices.

So as much as she wanted to believe that was the evidence they needed to get the judge to throw this case out, she knew they still needed to find another suspect as well. She couldn't simply sit back and pretend that clearing her own name was enough. The more evidence they could find, the better.

She glanced at the time and saw it was already past five o'clock.

If she had to guess, Brandon had already talked to Talen. Her dad's former associate had probably left the office by now.

She picked up the phone to call Brandon, to tell him the news that she could possibly have an alibi.

But when she dialed his number, the phone simply rang and rang and rang.

Her stomach tightened.

Was that because Brandon was still meeting with Talen?

Or was it because something had happened?

———

"Rocco . . ." Brandon muttered as he leaned back. "We're going to have to be very careful right now."

"That's possibly the understatement of the year." Rocco stared forward as the SUV teetered again.

The other car squealed away.

As it did, sirens sounded in the distance. Were they already headed this way?

Had someone down below seen this happen and called emergency services? It seemed likely, considering they'd busted through the guardrail and the concrete border.

That kind of thing tended to draw people's attention.

Brandon's phone rang, but he didn't dare move to answer it.

Not now.

Brandon sucked in another breath as the vehicle rocked back and forth.

All they needed was one wind gust to send them toppling.

"We can crawl into the back and go out the hatch," Rocco suggested. "That's going to be our best bet. But we need to move very slowly."

"I agree." Brandon nodded. "You should go first."

Rocco shot him a look. "Are you sure?"

"Positive. You're heavier than I am. We've got this."

Brandon kept saying that. He said the words because he believed they were true. But even in believing they were true, there was a small niggle of doubt.

Slowly, Rocco undid his seatbelt. Then he carefully pushed his seat back and climbed into the back.

Every time he moved, the SUV moved with him.

Dear Lord, help us now. Please. Because I'm no good to Finley if I'm dead. I have to clear her name.

Rocco reached the back, and Brandon hit the button to open the rear hatch.

As he did, the weight of the vehicle shifted again.

Brandon felt the SUV begin to tip forward.

CHAPTER
EIGHTEEN

JUST AS THE SUV started to lurch forward, it stopped.

Brandon glanced back at Rocco as he sat on the back of the vehicle. "Your weight back there seems to be helping."

"Let's hope." Rocco reached out his hand. "Grab on. I don't know how much longer this is going to hold."

At his words, more concrete crumbled from beneath the front of the vehicle.

The SUV shifted again.

Wasting no time, Brandon lunged at Rocco and grabbed his hand.

Just as he did, the vehicle began to slide.

It toppled forward.

It *really* toppled this time.

In the blink of an eye, the SUV disappeared from

beneath Brandon just as Rocco jerked him onto the concrete floor of the parking garage.

Brandon landed with a painful thud and sucked in a shallow breath as he tried to comprehend what had just happened.

They had gotten out in time. They were alive.

He only prayed no one had been underneath when the vehicle landed.

He rushed to the edge of the parking garage and glanced down at the crowd below.

They'd scattered and, from the looks of things, no one was hurt.

Thank God.

"Are you okay?" Brandon turned back to study Rocco.

His friend looked just as disheveled as he felt. "I'm fine. But someone wanted to kill us."

"More like they wanted to kill me." His jaw hardened at the thought.

Rocco's eyes narrowed. "Why would someone want to kill you?"

"I think it goes back to Finley. They want to make her suffer."

"Who could hate her so much?"

Brandon's jaw tightened. "That's what I keep asking myself."

"It has to be someone who thinks this is personal."

Brandon couldn't argue with his friend's assessment.

This went beyond anything business.

Someone had a personal vendetta against Finley and was determined to ruin her life.

Brandon had a feeling they wouldn't stop until they got what they wanted.

————

Finley gripped the phone and tried not to let worry overtake her thoughts.

But Brandon hadn't answered, and he hadn't called her back yet. She prayed he was okay.

As she waited for him to return her call—she decided she'd let at least fifteen minutes pass before she tried him again. She found a laptop she'd left at Blackout and opened it.

The device was charged.

She thought about her idea of getting into people's computers.

Should she even attempt it? Or was it a terrible idea?

She couldn't be sure.

But she was starting to feel desperate.

If she did nothing, she might spend the rest of her life in prison.

She couldn't let that happen.

Maybe she could at least formulate some type of

phishing e-mail that might get her prime suspects to click on a link. But the people she was investigating were smart. So not just any phishing e-mail would work. It would need to sound legit.

If she went forward with this plan, she needed to really think it through if she wanted it to work.

Finley closed the computer and grabbed some paper and a pen instead. Then she began to jot down some ideas.

What kind of e-mail would make someone click on a link?

She tapped the pen against her lips in thought.

She would say maybe something from a bank, but that seemed all too typical as far as e-mail scams went.

It would need to be from someone they trusted. Someone they already knew.

What if it was an invitation to a party?

Finley knew most of the people well enough that she might be able to guess who in their circles could be having a party.

If she sent them an electronic invitation and they clicked on the link to find more details . . . that would give her the back door she needed.

Excitement thrummed through her.

If she decided to go through with this, that was what she'd do.

She began brainstorming people in each of her suspect's inner circles who might throw a party and what kind of gathering it might be, jotting notes along the way.

Halfway through brainstorming, her phone rang.

Relief filled her.

It was Brandon.

She quickly put the phone to her ear, anxious to hear how he was doing. "How did everything go? I was getting worried."

"Finley . . . you're never going to believe this." His voice sounded strained. "Someone just rammed into our SUV in the parking garage. They nearly sent us over the edge."

She gasped at his words, unsure if she'd heard correctly. "What? You're okay though, right?"

"Rocco and I are fine. We got out just in time."

That was a relief, at least. "Did the police catch the guy who did this?"

"They're looking for him. It was a green Charger, and it's going to have some damage on the hood. We're hopeful that maybe this person can be found."

Her thoughts continued to race. "Was someone following you today?"

"We didn't see anyone. But I suppose that's the only thing that makes sense. It's all a bit baffling."

Yes, it was. But thankfully, things had turned out okay. "I'm so glad you weren't injured. What are you going to do now?"

"We just talked to Colton, and he's going to send someone here to pick us up. There's no need to get a rental since there's nowhere to return it on Lantern Beach. I'm not sure when we'll be back."

"All I'm concerned about is that you're safe." She meant those words. She only wanted Brandon to be okay in the middle of this horrible storm.

"I'm fine." His voice softened. "Don't worry about me."

That was easier said than done. Especially considering he'd almost been killed at a parking garage. She didn't even want to know what floor he'd been parked on.

"I can't talk a lot right now because the police have more questions for me," Brandon continued. "But I just wanted to let you know what was going on."

"Thank you. I love you, Brandon." Her throat burned as she said the words.

"I love you too."

She ended the call and pressed the phone against her heart.

What if the person who'd rammed into their vehicle had succeeded? What if someone managed to push both Brandon and Rocco over the side of that building, plunging them to their deaths?

Finley pressed her eyes shut, unable to do anything except pray.

But was God even listening? Or was He still trying to teach her some kind of lesson she had no desire to learn?

CHAPTER
NINETEEN

AFTER BRANDON and Rocco talked to the police, Brandon turned to Rocco. "We've got a lot of time to kill right now."

"What are you suggesting?" Rocco asked.

"I'm wondering if we should follow Talen when he leaves work."

"How do you know he hasn't already left work?"

"Because I slipped the doorman some money to text me when he left."

"Really?" Rocco nodded slowly. "Smart thinking."

"I have a few good ideas every now and then."

"Just one more thing we haven't thought of. We don't have a car."

"I have a friend in the area that we could call."

Rocco looked skeptical. "We don't need to involve anyone else in this."

"We don't have to tell him everything—we can be subtle. We're known for being subtle, right?"

A smile tugged at Rocco's lips. "Yeah, right."

Finally, Rocco shrugged. "What do we have to lose?"

Brandon didn't bother to answer that question.

Instead, they paced away from the scene of the crime. The police had cordoned off the area and would be here a while collecting evidence. But the cops had told Brandon and Rocco that they were free to go. There was nothing in the vehicle they needed, so they had no reason to stick around.

As they left, the two of them paused near a stairwell and Brandon dialed an old friend who worked in the area. Diego Martinez, another former SEAL, was a paramilitary contractor who consulted with Hollywood on the side. He said he was available and could help them out, promising to be there in ten minutes.

Right on cue, Diego pulled up in a black Jeep. He met Brandon and Rocco on the second level of the parking garage, which had now emptied out considerably. This was where Talen's car was parked—they'd done their research.

Brandon and Rocco climbed into Diego's Jeep, and they made small talk as they waited. Diego was an entertainer, someone who always told the best stories. And he'd always been up for anything.

Brandon was thankful for that right now.

He sat in the front seat with his friend, and Rocco sat in the back beside some dry cleaning.

Only five minutes later, Brandon's phone buzzed.

Talen was leaving.

Perfect timing.

Several minutes later, he exited the building using a pedestrian bridge that crossed to the parking garage. Brandon ducked lower in the Jeep so he wouldn't be spotted.

But through the car window, he saw Talen climbing into a black Lexus parked only a few spaces down from them.

"We need you to follow that car," Brandon said.

"You got it," Diego said.

This could all be nothing.

This guy could end up going straight home, and this whole plan could be a royal waste of time.

But maybe it wouldn't be.

———

Finley hadn't even been at Blackout for eight hours, and already this room was beginning to feel like a prison. Normally, she enjoyed being here. Spending time with Brandon and their friends.

She knew she could wander out of her living space and go to the cafeteria or the lounge area at the Daniel Oliver Building. But she also knew she wasn't ready to face other people and to answer their questions. Staying in this room seemed safer.

A couple of her friends had stopped by, and she'd chatted with them a few minutes before feigning exhaustion. But, as silence filled the room, she heard the crowd outside.

They were still there in full force, voicing their disapproval of Finley.

She frowned at the sound of them.

She had to do something to distract herself. Yet she couldn't get the conversation with Brandon out of her head.

He could have been killed.

And he'd done nothing wrong.

She couldn't stand the thought of that.

Finley couldn't wait to have him back here. To see him with her own eyes. To hold him.

She stole a glance at her laptop as it rested on the coffee table.

She had been stealing glances at the device every few minutes. She'd been contemplating her idea.

Clearly, there was no time to waste right now.

She opened her computer and began to formulate one of those invitations she'd written out by hand—a paper that she would burn in the kitchen sink as soon as she was done.

The stakes were just going to get higher again.

But if they didn't find answers, then Brandon might be killed.

She couldn't live with herself if that happened.

Finley knew she had to do whatever it took to keep Brandon safe.

She began typing the letter and developing the link she needed to access their computers, all while praying she didn't regret this.

CHAPTER
TWENTY

"WHO DO you think that guy is?" Brandon nodded out the window from the parked SUV.

"That's a good question." Rocco stared ahead as they watched Talen meet with a man at a park.

They both wore business suits and looked out of place in their professional attire.

Something about this whole meeting seemed too far-fetched for his liking.

"Maybe we should confront them." Brandon's thoughts turned over as he tried to think this through.

He didn't recognize this guy. The man was probably in his thirties, if Brandon had to guess, and tall with light-brown hair and confident movements.

"I'm not sure that's the way you're going to get any answers here." Rocco's lips flickered down in a frown.

His friend had a point. "For now, let's watch them for another moment."

"Sounds good," Diego muttered. "I'm just along for the ride. Or for the drive, I should say."

They continued to watch, waiting for anything that might signal what was going on.

Brandon's back straightened when he saw Talen hand the other man a piece of paper.

The man glanced around before sliding it into his coat pocket.

Then both Talen and the man he'd met with went their separate ways.

Definitely suspicious.

Brandon raised his phone and took a picture of the man. He wanted to know who the guy was.

"So do we follow that guy?" Rocco pointed toward the man Talen had met.

If they had two vehicles, Brandon would suggest they split up and follow both of them.

But they didn't, so he had to make a decision.

"We know who Talen is. Let's follow this other guy," Brandon said. "I want to know who he is. I want to know what that exchange was just about."

"Then let's go."

Brandon's heart pounded in his ears. One way or another, he was going to find some answers.

———

Finley sent three emails.

She hoped she didn't regret this, but she had to try.

Now she had to wait to see if anyone took the bait and clicked on the link she'd sent.

As she finished, she stood and stretched.

She glanced at the patio doors on one side of her apartment.

She'd largely avoided them.

But right now, it was dark outside, and she hadn't heard the crowd jeering for a while.

Maybe they had gone home for the night.

Or maybe that was wishful thinking.

She paced over toward the doors.

She thought about it a moment before sliding the door open and stepping onto the small balcony.

The air tonight was crisp, and there was a light breeze. She closed her eyes and raised her face toward the wind, relishing the feel of it.

This wasn't the Maldives, but she was grateful for a safe place to stay.

She and Brandon had decided that once they were married, she would work remotely from the island. She would probably still have to go into the office a couple of days a week, sometimes more, sometimes less. But they'd worked everything out so they could be together as much as possible.

She had so been looking forward to starting their life together.

Now, everything felt like it was in jeopardy.

Her gut rumbled with displeasure at the thought.

She stared at the fence line beyond the Daniel Oliver Building to the place where the protesters had been earlier.

It appeared they were gone, but then she couldn't quite see the very front of the property from her position.

At once, a series of pops filled the air.

She sucked in a breath and sank to the floor.

Was someone shooting at her?

It sounded like gunfire.

Her heart pounded harder at the thought.

Then she waited for whatever would happen next.

CHAPTER
TWENTY-ONE

BRANDON HAD the license plate number of the man Talen had met with, and he ran it through the system as Diego followed the man through the city.

He was currently waiting for the results.

He needed to know who this guy was.

What he wouldn't do to figure out what was on that paper in the guy's pocket.

Finally, the man parked in front of a luxury apartment building near downtown Norfolk. Diego pulled in several spaces behind him.

Just then, the results Brandon needed popped onto his screen. "This guy's name is Todd Watkins. He works for another tech company that specializes in artificial intelligence."

Rocco rubbed his beard. "The name doesn't ring any bells with me."

"Me either."

Brandon watched as the man climbed out and locked his car. Todd started toward the apartment building.

Brandon needed to act. And if he was going to act, it needed to be now. Otherwise, he was going to miss the perfect opportunity.

"I'll be back." Brandon grabbed the door handle and opened it.

Before his friends could stop him, he hopped out and grabbed some dry-cleaning Diego had hanging in the back seat. "I need to borrow these."

"Whatever you need, bruh," Diego called.

Then he hurried toward the apartment building in the distance, purposefully moving frantically. He held up the dry cleaning so it wouldn't drag the ground.

With the clothing blocking his line of sight, he ran right into Todd—on purpose, of course.

"Hey, what are you doing, man?" Brandon said as they collided. "Pay attention!"

"Me?" Todd's eyebrows knit together as he bristled. "You were the one who ran into me!"

Brandon reached down to grab the clothes from the sidewalk. As he stood, he let out a long breath as if composing himself. "Look, you're right. Sorry, man. I guess I've got too much on my mind and wasn't paying attention."

Todd stared at Brandon another moment, his eyes cold and icy.

Then he nodded curtly and kept going.

That was fine.

Because Brandon had been able to reach into Todd's pocket.

He'd grabbed that piece of paper Talen had slipped to Todd.

Brandon clenched the note as he hurried back to the SUV and hopped inside. That whole charade hadn't been for nothing.

"What was that about?" Rocco glanced at him, confusion in his gaze.

Brandon opened his hand and showed him the paper. "This."

————

With the sound of those pops still fresh in her ears, Finley rushed inside from the balcony, shut the door, and called Colton.

"We heard the noise also, and we're checking it out right now," Colton rushed.

"Thank you." She ended the call and gripped the phone in her hands.

What if she'd been shot at?

But . . . why hadn't she heard anything break? If someone had fired at her, there would be evidence of some bullets, right?

She didn't know.

But she was shaken.

Finley pressed herself against the wall and out of sight as she waited to hear back from Colton.

This nightmare was never going to end, was it?

No, Finley couldn't think like that.

She had to keep her hopes up.

She'd always been a doer. She got that trait from her father. They'd both liked to stay busy and weren't the type to sit around and twiddle their thumbs.

But now, Finley's life had been forced to a grinding halt, and she hated it.

Finally, about thirty minutes after she'd heard those pops, a knock sounded at her door. "Finley, it's Colton."

She opened the door and let him inside.

He paused near the entry. "I wanted to give you an update in person. There was someone outside the gates. We caught him. That wasn't gunfire. Thankfully, it was fireworks. Someone was just trying to scare you."

Finley shivered and rubbed her arms, still upset despite the update. "It worked."

Colton's expression softened. "I know, and I'm sorry. We do have guards around this place twenty-four seven. No one should be able to get in. But in the meantime, I suggest you stay inside just in case somebody gets any crazy ideas."

Finley agreed and talked to Colton a couple more minutes before he left. Then she shut the door, locked it, plopped on the couch, and picked up her laptop.

She stared at her computer in her lap before opening it to see if there were any updates on those invitations she'd sent out.

Her plan seemed like a long shot, but someone might go for it.

She logged on and saw that she did have a result.

Her breath caught.

Someone had clicked on the link she sent.

Ryan Hold.

Now, if she worked quickly enough then maybe she'd get inside his computer without him knowing. Then she could figure out if he was the one who'd done this to her.

CHAPTER
TWENTY-TWO

"WHAT ARE THESE NUMBERS?" Brandon stared at the paper as he sat in the SUV, the dim overhead light offering a gentle illumination.

Rocco peered over his shoulder at the paper. "Maybe it's a bank account. There are too many digits to be a phone number."

Brandon continued to stare, his mind racing. "Could this be an IP address? There are no periods between the numbers but . . . it could be."

"Whatever those numbers are, this makes Talen look very suspicious." Rocco leaned back and crossed his arms.

"I agree," Brandon said.

Rocco let out a breath. "We still have two hours to kill. What should we do now?"

Brandon knew exactly what he wanted to do.

He'd been wrestling with whether or not it was the best decision, however.

But this was no time to be hesitant—the stakes were too high.

"I want to talk to Talen again," Brandon announced.

Rocco's eyes widened as he turned to him. "Do you really think that's a good idea?"

"I don't know if it's a good idea or not. But we don't have a lot of time here. If these numbers somehow correspond with what's happening or prove that there's some type of payout, I want to know."

"You don't think Talen is just going to admit to anything, do you?" Diego cast a skeptical glance over his shoulder.

"No, I know that would be too easy," Brandon admitted. "But we should at least try."

No one said anything for a moment until Diego asked, "Do you think you can get his address?"

"Let me see what I can do," Brandon muttered as he pulled out his phone and began typing.

———

Finley was rusty at this. Really, she was more of a businessperson. But she'd learned a lot of the tricks of the trade since she'd taken over as CEO at Embolden. She had to understand exactly what her engineers were doing before she could promote some of the products they were developing.

It took several tries, but she finally managed to access Ryan's computer.

A sense of victory rushed through her.

Her entire screen transformed into a view of Ryan's computer.

Now she just had to figure out where to begin poking around in order to find the information she needed.

Had the FBI already gone through his computer and files? Or was Ryan not even on their radar?

Most likely, he hadn't been on their radar. Only Finley was.

But Ryan was a smart guy. If he'd been involved in any of this, he wouldn't make that information easy to find. The stakes were too high.

But she knew about a couple of apps people often used to hide their information.

Was that what he would do?

Finley could also try to figure out a way to check his bank account and his emails as well as his internet searches. Each of those things would help her form a more complete picture of what Ryan may or may not have been up to.

But this would take some time.

She brewed herself some coffee, knowing she'd need to stay awake for a while. There was no way she could sleep, not when she had this opportunity placed in front of her.

After Finley fixed her coffee and sat down and took a sip, she lifted a prayer. She knew what she was doing was illegal. She knew it could send her back to jail. She knew it could make her look guilty.

But she'd been pushed into a corner. She had no other choice but to find out the information she needed this way.

With that thought in mind, Finley began searching through Ryan's emails.

CHAPTER
TWENTY-THREE

FIVE MINUTES LATER, Brandon found Talen's address.

Fifteen minutes after that, Brandon, Rocco, and Diego pulled up to a massive Georgian-style house in an affluent neighborhood.

The size of the house was surprising, considering most of Talen's business ventures had failed.

But if this man had taken money from the Chinese government in return for secrets, then that would explain how he'd been able to afford this place.

"While I go talk to him, can one of you check how long ago Talen bought this house?" Brandon asked as he stared at the place. Two of the front windows were lit, but the rest of the house remained dark. However, Talen's car was in the driveway.

Brandon thought the man should be here.

"I can do that." Diego reached into his bag and grabbed a laptop.

"Perfect." Brandon turned to Rocco. "I'd like to talk to him by myself."

Rocco raised his eyebrows. "You sure? I don't mind going with you."

"The more I can keep you guys out of this, the better," Brandon said. "I really don't know where this is going to lead. Besides, if we both go, he might think we're trying to intimidate him. What I really want is simply to have a conversation."

Rocco stared at him another moment before nodding. "Okay then. If that's what you want."

Brandon dragged in a deep breath before opening his door. *Here goes nothing.*

He strode up the long driveway toward an enormous porch and pressed on the doorbell.

It was getting late, and he knew many people probably wouldn't answer at this time of the evening.

But only a few seconds later, Talen did.

He still wore his suit, though his tie had been loosened, and he had a glass in his hand halfway full of an amber-colored liquid.

His eyes widened when he saw Brandon standing there.

"You have a lot of nerve coming here. We finished this conversation earlier at my office. I have nothing more to say." Talen started to shut the door.

Brandon shoved out his foot to block the door. "Please, I only need a few minutes."

Talen gave him a scathing glare as he stared at Brandon's foot. "What do you think you're doing? Remove yourself from my doorway before I call the police."

Brandon stepped closer and lowered his voice, knowing he was on borrowed time right now. "I saw you meeting with Todd Watkins. I saw you give him a piece of paper, and I know you're up to something dirty. I know you might even be behind Finley's arrest."

Talen's eyes widened, and he glanced behind Brandon as if looking for someone else. The police maybe? Momentary panic raced through his gaze.

Finally, he turned back to Brandon.

"I would never do that sort of thing," Talen seethed. "You're wrong."

"Then what were you doing at that secret meeting? Why did you give these numbers to Todd Watkins?" Brandon held up the sheet of paper he'd stolen from Todd.

Talen's skin dropped three shades. "How did you get that?"

"I have my ways." A sense of satisfaction stretched through Brandon when he realized he had Talen exactly where he wanted him.

"Is Todd okay?" Talen rushed.

"He's fine. He probably doesn't even know he's

missing this yet." Brandon leveled his gaze. "Now I need you to start talking before I call the FBI."

Talen let out a long breath of defeat before nodding. "Fine. Come inside. I don't want to have this conversation out here."

Brandon cast a glance back at his friends before stepping inside Talen's house.

Talen didn't offer him a seat or a drink. They would have this conversation in the foyer, it appeared.

Talen's pinched expression deepened. "It's not what you think."

"Are you sure? Because what I think is that you set up Finley and are getting payouts from the Chinese for doing so. That's probably how you bought this place and are keeping your business afloat."

"I'll have you know that this place was left to me by my parents." His nostrils flared. "I come from old money, and all I ever wanted to do was to make my dad proud. But none of my businesses have taken off the way I wanted."

"Tell me more." Brandon crossed his arms, considering the man's words very carefully.

Talen let out a breath and ran a hand through his hair. "The truth is that I'm trying to merge my company with another one, the one that Todd works for."

Brandon hadn't expected that revelation, but it was a good start. "Why are you trying to do that?"

"Because Smart Intelligence is in the red. I thought we'd have more investors on board at this point, but we don't. I can't afford to go under again."

"Even if that's the truth, why the secret meeting?" Brandon's mind still raced through the possibilities.

A faint sheen appeared on Talen's forehead. "Not everyone at Todd's company is on board. I've been trying to persuade him to convince the rest of the board members."

"So you met with him in secret?" Brandon was still trying to put everything together.

"Todd doesn't want anyone else to know that the two of us have been talking. He says it would look suspicious. That's why we met in private like we did."

"And the piece of paper you gave him?"

More sweat appeared across his skin. "The numbers represent the IP address of a computer Todd can log onto in order to see everything he needs to know about my company's financials. I didn't want any type of paper trail that connected us online. That's why I wrote it out for him to use. Going old school, as kids say these days, can be beneficial."

Brandon would take everything this man said with a grain of salt. "It seems very clandestine to go through all that just for a company merger."

"My livelihood is on the line. If this merger doesn't happen, I'm going to be bankrupt. The success of this means everything to me. That's why I'm trying to convince Todd to go forward with the merger."

"How are you trying to convince him?" Brandon prodded. "Did you slip him something under the table maybe?"

Talen scowled but didn't answer.

His silence was answer enough.

A more complete story solidified in Brandon's mind.

"If you're so desperate for this money, then who's to say you didn't try to sell secrets to China?" Brandon stared at him, looking for any sign of deception in the man's eyes.

Talen locked his gaze with Brandon's. "Even if I wanted to do that—which I don't—it pains me to say this, but I'm not nearly smart enough to know how to do the things that would be required."

"You have the means to hire people," Brandon reminded him.

His gaze darkened as if he didn't appreciate Brandon's interrogation. "Maybe. But it wouldn't be very wise if I did that. The more people involved, the better the chance I'd be caught. Besides, I'm not in favor of selling US secrets. In my opinion, China is going to be the ruin of this country. Why would I want to help a regime that's ultimately going to lead to my demise?"

Brandon stared at Talen another moment.

Brandon didn't think that this man was lying about this, but he would still need to verify Talen's story.

If his story checked out then Brandon could mark Talen off his list of suspects.

But that left him back at square one . . . the last place he wanted to be.

———

Just as Finley hoped, she found some deleted emails on Ryan's computer.

She felt as if she'd hit the jackpot.

Most of the messages were inconsequential. Ryan had apparently joined a website where he met women, some of them married. He'd hidden those emails, no doubt because he was married himself.

Those secrets were disgusting, but they didn't mean he was guilty of setting Finley up.

Then she found some emails Ryan had sent to several prominent news reporters.

Emails that promised dirt on Finley and her company.

Her back went ramrod straight as she read them.

Even though Ryan had said he was having medical procedures at the time these actions of treason happened, Finley needed to look at that time-line again. If these messages had been sent in May, then maybe he *could* have done all of this before his brain tumor diagnosis.

Because this definitely proved he was trying to set Finley up. To destroy her.

Her resolve to find answers hardened.

She would keep digging and see if she could find any emails Ryan sent to Chinese officials. No doubt they would be encrypted so that would require more work.

But this seemed to be the evidence Finley needed to prove he was out to get her.

Why would Ryan hate her so much?

She clicked on a few more emails and some social media messages.

That's when she found her answer buried in some messages Ryan had sent to an old college friend.

Apparently, when Finley fired him, Ryan had been devastated. Humiliated. And he'd hit rock bottom.

Had hitting rock bottom made something snap inside him? Made him boil with anger and long for vengeance?

It was a possibility.

Either way, Finley felt like Ryan was her best lead.

She needed to keep looking into him.

For now, she couldn't wait for Brandon to get back.

So much had happened today.

And she couldn't forget the fact that Brandon had nearly been killed.

Because of her.

Regret twisted in her gut.

She glanced at her watch and saw it was almost midnight.

What time had Brandon said he might be back?

She couldn't remember for sure.

Whatever hour that was, Finley would wait up for him.

Somewhere along the way, he'd become her rock. And she needed him right now before this storm blew her away.

CHAPTER
TWENTY-FOUR

BRANDON HAD GOTTEN a text from Finley as he headed back to Lantern Beach.

> Wake me up when you're back. I don't care what time it is.

He was anxious to see her too. Thankfully, Colton had sent a helicopter for them. Otherwise, they'd be driving through most of the night, which wouldn't be ideal.

When they arrived back at Blackout Headquarters, Brandon thanked Rocco for his help. Then he headed upstairs to Finley's room.

He couldn't wait to see her. To hear how she was doing and how her day had gone. To share his updates.

There were some conversations best had in person and not over the phone.

He reached her door and started to knock when it opened.

Finley burst from her apartment and threw her arms around his neck.

He let out a little chuckle as her hair tickled his cheek. "I'm happy to see you too."

"I thought you were never going to get back. I've been so worried about everything." Her words came out as a whisper.

He kissed her forehead. "I'm here. And I'm fine."

He took her arm and led her inside, closing the door behind him. Then they went to the couch, and she curled beside him, resting her head on his shoulder.

He wrapped his arms around her, relishing this moment.

"It sounds as if you've had a rough day also," he murmured into her hair.

She'd already told him about the fireworks earlier, and he could only imagine how that must have frightened her—especially in light of everything else that had happened.

"This has all been a lot for me." Her voice sounded lackluster—not surprising, considering everything going on.

"Understandably."

"Did you discover anything?" Finley murmured.

He told her about Talen, and she seemed to process each new tidbit he shared.

"So you really don't think he's guilty?" Finley pulled away from Brandon enough to look him in the eye.

He shrugged. "My gut tells me he's not. I'm not saying he's a Boy Scout or anything, but when he said he doesn't have the capabilities of doing this to you, I think he's telling the truth. A lot of the new technology he's been trying to develop are things he's hired other people to create."

"And he's too smart to get other people involved with something like this." Her lips tugged down on the edges. "Other people would sell him out for the right amount of money."

"Exactly."

Finley stared at Brandon a moment, almost as if she wanted to say something. He waited, but she didn't speak.

But as he looked into her eyes, another thought hit him—maybe his craziest thought of all.

"Maybe we should just elope," he murmured as he gently pushed a hair behind her ear. "Forget about a big ceremony. Forget about all the planning. We should just get married. Now." He paused. "Maybe not *right now* . . . but tomorrow. I hate to think that this incident is going to alter the course of our future."

Finley stared at him, her eyes widening with surprise. "You really want to do that?"

"I'd do it in a heartbeat." Brandon's gaze locked with hers. "What do you say?"

———

Finley considered Brandon's suggestion. Eloping?

On one hand, the idea sounded glorious. She knew she wanted to be Brandon's wife. She had no doubt about that.

But on the other hand, marrying him would ensure he was tied to this scandal.

And she couldn't do that to him.

She remembered what Agent Bills had said to her when she was being interrogated. *One day, your fiancé is going to thank us for stopping this marriage before it ever happened.*

What if he was right?

Because, deep inside, she feared he was.

Finley reached up and ran her fingers across Brandon's face, feeling the stubble from a day's growth on his chin. "I think that's sweet. But when we get married, I want it to be the happiest day of our lives. I'm not really sure that's what we're going to experience right now. Not with everything going on."

"We could have a bigger ceremony later . . ." Brandon shrugged, tension stretching through his voice. He was being strong for her, but this whole thing had been hard on him also, hadn't it?

The truth was, there was a good chance it would only get more difficult.

"I don't want to rush this." It was really sweet that Brandon was trying to think of her like this. Part of her did just want to say yes.

But Finley would regret that later.

Especially if Brandon suffered any more because of her.

She knew him. Knew he would stick with her for better or for worse. She had to consider that.

This whole situation reminded her of a childhood incident. She'd dived into a friend's swimming pool, assuming it was deep. She was actually in the shallow end.

She could have broken her neck, but she hadn't. Still, she'd spent three weeks in the hospital trying to recover from the neck injuries she did sustain.

Her mother had gotten misty-eyed every time she talked about it, up until the day she died.

Nothing was as it seemed, and the end result could be deadly.

That's why Finley had to be observant and double-check every detail for accuracy. Why she had to weigh every option.

There was no room for mistakes here.

And she wasn't sending Brandon to dive into this deadly pool first. Just like she couldn't tell him yet about hacking into Ryan's computer. It was better if he didn't know, just in case the whole thing went south.

Instead, she slipped her arms around his neck. "Let's just wait. Everything is too fresh right now. There's too much pressure."

He frowned but nodded. "I understand."

Brandon stared at her another moment before planting a slow and easy kiss on her lips.

For just a moment, Finley's worries disappeared.

If only a kiss would make her concerns disappear for good.

But life, unfortunately, wasn't that easy.

They still had an enormous battle in front of them.

CHAPTER
TWENTY-FIVE

BRANDON WOKE up the next morning with a start.

His whole body felt stiff and sore.

When he glanced around, he realized he and Finley had fallen asleep on her couch. His arms were still around her, and she was still snuggled against his chest.

The last thing he remembered was the two of them talking.

It had been late, and they'd both been exhausted. They must have both drifted to sleep and gotten some much needed rest.

As he shifted, Finley began to stir.

She looked up, a sleepy smile across her face when she realized Brandon was with her.

"Good morning. I didn't realize . . ." She pulled

away from him slightly, seeming just as surprised as he was.

"We were both tired."

"I always rest better when I know you're near."

"Me too." He kissed the top of her head. "If only we could stay like this all day."

"If only."

Brandon sighed and ran a hand over his face. Then he stood and stretched his stiff muscles. "How about some breakfast?"

"Breakfast sounds great." She flashed a grateful smile.

He wandered into the kitchen and pulled out some eggs and bacon. Finley got herself cleaned up as he cooked, and when she returned from the shower, breakfast waited for her on the table.

Brandon had to admit that he was starting to like this new natural look on Finley. She usually wore business attire and had every hair in place. But ever since her arrest, she'd been wearing joggers and T-shirts.

Finley would look good however she dressed, and Brandon appreciated all those different looks on her. She didn't show this vulnerable side to very many people, however, and he felt honored to know she let him inside.

She sat down, and they joined hands to pray. Then she took a sip of her coffee.

"This looks wonderful." She nodded toward the plate in front of her.

"I think you've already lost some weight since all this happened." He'd been worried about her—for more than one reason. "I figured you could use a good meal."

She didn't deny his words.

"What do you have going on today?" Finley switched the subject and set her coffee on the table.

He pulled out a chair across from her and shrugged. "I'm glad you asked. I think I might go talk to Victor."

"Victor?" She raised her eyebrows. "I wasn't expecting that."

"Well, if we've cleared Talen and Ryan—"

"Both of them?" she interrupted as Ryan's image flittered through her mind.

"As far as I'm concerned."

Finley frowned, wondering how much she should say.

She remained quiet—for now.

"That only leaves Victor from the original list we put together," Brandon continued. "And Talen said the man stopped by to ask questions about you a couple of weeks ago."

"What?"

"Sorry. I thought I told you. He stopped by to talk to Talen. Said he wanted to surprise you with a photo book with pictures of your father."

She balked. "Why would he say that?"

"Maybe he was fishing for information. Talen said he had a strange look in his eyes. He refused to give him any photos—said it was too invasive."

"That gives me the creeps." A shiver raked through her.

"Rightfully so. We can look into him."

Finley nibbled on her bottom lip a moment as if she wanted to say something.

She'd had that same look last night.

Exactly what was going through her mind? Brandon knew her well enough to know there was something there. But he didn't want to push. She'd tell him when she was ready.

She took a bite of her bacon—crisp, just the way she liked it. Not soggy or limp.

And her eggs were perfect also—over medium with a soft, slightly runny yolk. He'd learned her preferences.

"I think we should still look into Ryan," Finley finally said. "I sketched out a timeline, and I believe he could have done some of this before his brain tumor diagnosis."

Brandon tilted his head in surprise. "Is that right?"

She nodded. "I had a lot of time to think about it yesterday . . . to do a little research, so to speak."

A little research? What did that mean? Did he dare ask?

Maybe later.

"If you think we should look more into Ryan, then we can do that," he finally said. "I can just as easily go talk to him today as I can Victor."

She swallowed hard as their gazes met. She clearly still had something on her mind.

"I'd like to go with you," she announced.

Without thinking, Brandon swung his head back and forth. "I don't think that's a good idea. I think it's a *terrible* idea, actually."

Finley reached across the table and squeezed his hand. "Please. I'm going crazy here. There's a chance I could spend the rest of my life in prison. Yet I feel like I'm in a holding cell right now."

Her words resonated with him, and he felt his resolve weaken.

Brandon could understand what she was saying. This might be Finley's last touch of freedom for a while, and she was spending it locked inside a room, unable to leave.

No, don't think like that. She's going to be cleared.

But the only way she'd be cleared was if they found the real culprit.

He hesitated another moment before saying, "Okay. If you want to go with me then we'll arrange it so that you can go with me."

Finley's shoulders slumped with relief. "Thank you. I figure the best way to get in and out of this place is by helicopter at this point. I can pay for any of these travels that you want to do. I don't want you guys to have to foot my bill."

"Footing the bill is the least of my concerns right now." His words felt like an understatement.

As soon as they finished breakfast, Brandon would need to set some things up if they wanted to talk to Ryan Hold today. Finley had good instincts, and if she wanted to talk to him, then that was what they should do.

He only hoped the man might provide some answers.

————

Finley felt relief sweep through her.

Brandon had agreed to let her go along. She'd been sure he'd put up more of a fight. He was so intent on keeping her safe.

But maybe a safe life wasn't what God intended for her. Maybe God wasn't picking on her. Maybe He just had bigger plans.

What Brandon had told her a couple of nights ago was right. Most of the people she admired the most had been through hard times—and instead of feeling sorry for themselves, they'd fought to keep their heads above water.

She had no choice but to aim for that also.

Besides, the thought of spending another day alone inside this apartment was enough to make her feel like she was losing her mind. Finley needed to be out there doing something. Finding answers. Fighting for herself.

Fighting for Brandon.

After they finished eating, she cleaned up while Brandon escaped to his own apartment to get ready.

Her heart raced as she remembered the research she'd done while Brandon had been gone.

Finley really should tell him about what she'd done with those online invitations.

But she didn't want to pull him any deeper into her mess.

Yet keeping him in the dark could be just as dangerous.

Her inner conflict warred inside her.

When Brandon arrived back at her place thirty minutes later ready to go, Finley knew what she needed to do.

She gripped his arm as she looked up at him from the doorway. "I need to tell you something first."

He narrowed his eyes with curiosity and stepped inside, closing the door behind him. "Of course. Anything."

She knew she needed to dive right in or she might change her mind. "I sent out a phishing email to the people I suspected could be behind this. Whenever any of them click on the link, it gives me access to their personal computers."

"What?" His voice rose breathlessly. "Isn't that illegal?"

She nibbled on her lip before nodding. "It is. And I regret that. But it was the only way I could think of to get some answers. The FBI isn't even looking at these guys."

Brandon ran a hand through his hair and blinked several times. "I get that, but . . . if you're caught . . ."

"I know." She crossed her arms, the stress of the situation hitting her once again. "But I have to do something. I didn't want to ask anyone else to do this for me."

Brandon rubbed her arms, his gaze softening. "I'm glad you told me, even though part of me wishes you hadn't done this."

"I didn't want to tell you because I knew it was a risk and I didn't want to get you in any trouble. I don't want the FBI to have any reason to suspect you. And the way things are going right now . . ."

"You don't need to worry about me. I'll worry about myself."

"That's like me telling *you* not to worry about *me*."

He rested his hands on either side of her neck, his thumbs stroking along her jawline. "I just don't want anything else bad happening to you."

"I know, and I love you for that . . ."

"Did you discover anything? From Ryan's computer?"

Finley told him about the emails she'd found from Ryan to various news reporters.

His eyebrows flicked up. "That *is* very interesting."

"And that's why I think we should go talk to Ryan today."

"I agree." Brandon paused as their gazes locked. "But the next time you do something like this, tell me first. Okay?"

She nodded. "Okay."

A steady thumping noise sounded outside, growing louder and louder.

Brandon dropped his hands from her and nodded toward the door. "The helicopter's here. We need to get going."

CHAPTER
TWENTY-SIX

FINLEY AND BRANDON took off in the helicopter to Durham. She pushed down any nerves as she remembered that drone hitting the copter's blades as they'd landed in Lantern Beach earlier, and she prayed for safe travel.

The crowd outside Blackout hadn't thinned yet, and she wasn't sure how long they'd insist on coming out.

For now, she was grateful to get away.

They took off without issue and soared through the air.

Brandon had arranged for a rental vehicle to be waiting for them. As soon as they landed in Durham, they climbed inside the SUV.

Finley's phone rang.

It was Amanda.

Finley hesitated only a moment before answering, putting it on speaker so Brandon could also hear.

"Where are you?" Amanda demanded, her voice terse, making her sound irritated.

"It's not important." Again, Finley figured the less people knew the better.

"You didn't leave the state, did you? That would break the terms of your bail."

"I didn't leave the state," Finley told her. "How did you even know I left to go anywhere?"

"Because I came back to Lantern Beach. I talked to my partners, and they decided to handle things in Raleigh."

"You're back?" Finley's eyes widened with surprise. "I had no idea. If you'd told me, I would have stayed."

"If I'd known there was a possibility of you leaving, I would have mentioned it." Amanda sighed. "Just promise me you won't do anything foolish."

"I'm trying not to." Finley's jaw tightened. "Is there another reason you're calling?"

"I heard today that the prosecution found more evidence against you."

Her breath caught. "Did they say what kind of evidence?"

"Not yet. They're supposed to send something over tomorrow. I'll let you know when I find out what it is."

What kind of evidence had someone planted now?

———

As Brandon drove toward Ryan Hold's place, he ruminated on what Finley had done.

Part of him wished she hadn't gone so far as to send out those invitations. But another part of him knew it had been a smart move. He'd probably do the same thing in Finley's shoes if he had that kind of skill.

The fact that Finley had created personalized invitations from people she knew were in the recipient's lives was also a great move.

If she wasn't so good at what she did—running Embolden Tech—they could use someone of her skill set at Blackout.

But Brandon would never ask that of her. She loved carrying on her father's legacy, and he wouldn't want to take that from her.

On the other hand, her actions put her at risk. He didn't like that.

The GPS told him to make another turn, and he did so.

"So tell me more about Ryan." Brandon had done some research on the man himself, but nothing beat hearing from someone who'd actually interacted with him.

"I told you about his crazy behavior." Finley frowned as she glanced out the window. "But, really, he's practically a genius. He could have definitely figured out how to frame me and cover his steps."

Brandon drummed his thumbs on the steering wheel as he thought everything through. "So you're saying that there could be more information on his computer that you haven't found yet?"

"Exactly." She nodded assuredly. "I still have some more digging to do, but I haven't been able to yet."

"Did I read his file correctly and see that he's married?"

"That's right. His wife is Allison, and she seemed nice enough when I met her. She's a doctor, and she's probably the one who noticed the changes in his personality. Looking back and knowing now that he had a brain tumor, everything kind of makes sense."

"I can imagine." Brandon stared ahead at the suburban streets as they passed them headed toward Ryan's.

"However, when I dug into Ryan's computer, I also saw that he'd recently been on some online dating websites. For that reason, I suspect maybe their marriage has some struggles."

"I'd say." Brandon shook his head. "I'm liking this guy less and less all the time. Do they have any kids?"

"No, no kids. I don't think Ryan wants any children. At least, that's what I heard him say once in the breakroom."

Brandon's mind still raced as he tried to put together a more complete picture of who this guy was. "He's pretty young, right? Probably close to your age?"

"That's right. But he and his wife are both very focused on their careers, from what I remember."

Brandon soaked in all those facts. As he did, he glanced behind him. He needed to make sure they weren't being followed.

Someone seemed to be aware of their every move, and he didn't like the thought of that. He'd covered their tracks, and there was no way anyone could know where they were right now, especially since Finley had a new cell phone.

But he needed to remain on guard.

Finley directed him to stop in front of a bakery, where she ran inside to grab something. She returned a few minutes later with a box in her hands.

"It's a turtle cheesecake—Ryan's favorite," she explained. "I thought it would be a nice peace offering of sorts."

"Smart thinking."

Several minutes later, they pulled a stop in front of a newer craftsman-style house located on a large lot in an upper-class neighborhood.

Finley double-checked the address.

This was it—Ryan's house.

Brandon turned to Finley and studied her face. "Are you ready for this?"

"As ready as I'll ever be."

CHAPTER
TWENTY-SEVEN

FINLEY GRIPPED the cheesecake in one hand and rang the doorbell with the other. Then she waited.

What if she and Brandon had come all the way out here for nothing? Or if Ryan didn't answer?

But a few moments later, the door opened.

A woman wearing pink scrubs stood there. "Can I help you?"

"We're here to see Ryan," Finley said, plastering a pleasant smile on her face. "We're old friends."

The nurse, a black woman in her forties, eyed them both, almost as if surprised Ryan had any friends. "I don't know that he's up for visitors right now."

"I understand this has been a tough time. But I wanted to bring him some of his favorite food."

"Your names?"

"Finley Cooper and Brandon Hale."

The dubious look remained in the nurse's eyes. "Let me check with him and see. One moment."

She closed the door, keeping them outside.

Finley wondered for a moment if the woman would ever return or if she'd simply leave them out here.

A moment later, Ryan appeared at the door.

Finley's heart leapt into her throat at the sight of him.

He wore blue pajama bottoms, a white T-shirt, and a dark blue robe. He held a cane with his right hand, and a white bandage was wrapped around his head.

Even though she knew he could be guilty, compassion surged to the surface.

She couldn't imagine everything he'd been through.

"Finley . . ." His voice sounded dull yet surprised. "I wasn't expecting to see you here."

"This is my fiancé, Brandon." She held out the box in her hands. "I remembered how much you liked the cheesecake from the little place down the road. I brought you some."

He eyed the box suspiciously before glancing at his nurse. "Rosie, would you mind taking it to the kitchen and giving us a moment?"

"Of course." She took the bag and hurried away.

Finley glanced behind him. "Where is Allison?"

Ryan's gaze darkened. "She and I have split. That's all I care to say about that." He shifted. "Now, in light of everything that's happened, I can only assume you didn't come all the way out here to bring the cheesecake."

"I didn't," Finley admitted. "I know you're going through a difficult time health-wise right now, and I'm sorry to hear that. However, I heard through the grapevine that you contacted some reporters and wanted to do an exposé on me."

She halfway expected him to be angry or deny it.

Instead, his shoulders slumped. "Maybe we should sit down. Come on inside."

His words surprised Finley, but she obliged.

She was anxious to hear what he was about to say.

———

Finley and Brandon waited for Ryan to start.

He led them into an office area right off the foyer. The room was decorated with bookshelves along one wall, a dark rug, and a cozy leather loveseat with a matching chair.

Ryan slowly lowered himself into the chair, obviously still weak from his surgery. "I spoke to someone else about you earlier."

"I heard." Finley scowled when she remembered

hearing how Ryan had been gloating about Finley's misfortune.

"I'm sorry about that." Ryan's voice sounded dull. "I haven't been myself. However, the doctors said I should make a full recovery and be back to normal given some time."

"I'm glad to hear that. But did you just admit that you were happy about my being arrested?" Finley hadn't expected that.

"I was upset with you after you fired me. I'm not the type who gets fired. I'm the type who is pursued by four of the top ten leading tech companies in this country. I went to work for Embolden because I believed in what you guys were doing. To get fired was an ego bruise, to say the least."

"I didn't want to fire you," Finley reminded him. "I wanted to get you help."

He frowned. "I guess all along this brain tumor was affecting my personality. I just didn't realize it."

"What else did you do to get revenge on Finley after she let you go?" Brandon asked.

Ryan's eyes narrowed. "I didn't set her up as a traitor, if that's what you're asking. I'd never take things that far. I just wanted to mar her reputation a little bit."

"My understanding is that you contacted several reporters." Finley tried to choose her words wisely so Ryan wouldn't suspect she'd sent that email. "I'm kind of surprised that none of them took the bait."

"They did. I got some responses."

Finley had seen those. But there hadn't been any follow-up. Why was that?

"And what did you do then?" Finley asked.

His gaze darkened. "Then my wife left me, and I discovered I had a brain tumor. Suddenly, ruining you didn't seem that important."

Finley stared at him another moment, trying to decide whether or not she believed what he was saying.

CHAPTER
TWENTY-EIGHT

BRANDON WAITED until they were back in their SUV before he turned to Finley. "What do you think about what Ryan told us?"

"Unfortunately, I believe him." She frowned and crossed her arms. "I guess maybe I wanted him to be the bad guy because at least I'd have some answers. I don't think he is."

"I agree," Brandon said. "He was vengeful, but I don't think he took things that far. I made a call to Dr. Autumn Mercer yesterday as I was driving up to Norfolk, just to get her thoughts on the whole situation. She confirmed that sometimes when a person has a brain tumor in a certain area of the brain, it can change a person's personality."

"I've heard that before also." Finley rubbed a hand over her face. "I have to admit I kind of feel bad for the guy. I mean, even before his brain tumor was diagnosed. He was a bit arrogant. But he was also extremely smart."

"Maybe this whole situation will end up working out really well. Maybe it's giving him a new perspective. And he made it sound like doctors have said he would make a full recovery from this."

"It's true. So where does this leave us?"

He glanced at the time. "How about if we find a place we can have some lunch?"

Finley pointed to her face. "What if someone recognizes me?"

"I brought you a hat and some sunglasses. We can go somewhere quiet and hope for the best. And we can discuss our next plan of action over a burger and fries. How does that sound?"

"I'm surprisingly hungry, all things considered."

"I think I know just the place where we can eat. It's off the beaten path, and there's outdoor seating. We'll make sure you sit with your back to the crowd, and I think we'll be okay."

Finley nodded. "Going out to eat almost makes me feel normal."

"Hopefully, you'll be feeling a lot more of this normal feeling in the future."

She nodded. "I really hope so."

———

Just as Brandon had said, the restaurant he took her to was off the beaten path. It was surrounded by woods and a recreational lake. Mostly boaters stopped by to eat at the place, which had a country club feel.

While Brandon ordered, Finley found a seat slightly behind the corner, and she sat with her back toward the other patrons there. Her oversized baseball cap nicely concealed her face as did the sunglasses.

It was warm outside, but the sunshine felt good on her skin.

Once she and Brandon had their food and drinks —Finley had ordered some freshly squeezed lemonade that was the perfect mix of sweet and sour across her tongue—they finally started.

"So, we ruled out Talen first. And now Ryan. That only leaves Victor," Finley said. "But I have trouble thinking he'd go through all this just because I didn't want to see him anymore. I threw out his name initially because he was someone who said some pretty awful things about me. But he's an engineer by trade, and I'm just not sure I could see him taking it this far."

"I had Maddox look into him. It turns out Victor has been hiking in Alaska for the past two weeks."

Finley still wasn't ready to dismiss him. "That doesn't mean he couldn't have set this up back in May."

Brandon held his hamburger up, ready to take a bite. "That's true. I suppose when we dig into it, it makes sense that the person who's been coming at you since these accusations were unleashed could be different than the person who set you up."

Finley took a moment to process his words.

She knew what he was saying. Someone had set her up for treason. But her recent attacks may have been done by someone upset with her because of the accusations.

Suddenly, the hair on her arms rose, and she glanced around.

"What is it?" Brandon put his burger back on his plate and scanned everything around them.

"I can't help but feel like I'm being watched right now." She surveyed the area—the other patrons at the restaurant, boaters, a few people in a distant parking lot. No one seemed suspicious. But she couldn't shake the feeling. "Do you feel it too?"

He glanced around, his gaze scanning everything and everyone around them. "I don't see anyone suspicious. I'll keep my eyes open. In the meantime, let's finish this meal and get out of here."

Finley pulled her hat down lower and tried to eat.

CHAPTER
TWENTY-NINE

BRANDON DIDN'T LIKE the thought of anyone watching them here at the restaurant. He'd been careful when he left Ryan's house, and no one had followed them.

But that didn't mean they hadn't been discovered.

The list of suspects dwindled in his mind. Brandon had wanted to narrow it down, but he didn't want to narrow his list to zero.

But that was how it appeared this case was going.

He and Finley needed to talk about other possible suspects.

As they sat in the restaurant—other diners eating and some boaters jetting by on water skis—a new song began to play on the overhead.

"Can't Help Falling in Love."

They exchanged a glance.

Hearing the melody brought everything crashing

back. All the loss he and Finley had experienced because of this.

Brandon wanted to believe that one day things would go back to being the same between them.

But he needed to prepare himself for the possibility that they wouldn't.

This trial could stretch on for years. He'd seen it happen before.

And in the meantime, people would continue to go after Finley.

Finley's arrest wasn't something that would disappear off their radar as quickly as it had appeared.

Not in his experience, at least.

But he didn't tell Finley that.

She probably knew those facts already, but he didn't want to be the one to remind her.

"When I met you, I knew you were the man of my dreams," Finley started. "The way you swooped in and saved me from those men back in Ecuador took my breath away."

He swallowed hard. Because after that, he'd blown it.

Finley had been his target when he worked for the CIA. He hadn't expected to fall in love with her. By the time he'd realized that he had, he was in too deep.

He'd been certain Finley would never give him another chance. But she had.

Up until her arrest, he'd been the happiest he'd ever been.

"Our story isn't finished being written yet." His gaze met hers from across the table.

Finley cast him a soft smile—an almost grievous smile. "I hope not."

But she didn't sound that hopeful, and that realization made regret swirl inside him. He wanted to reassure her. But how could he?

Everything was on the line right now.

His phone rang and pulled him from the moment. He recognized the number and excused himself to answer. It was one of the vendors from the wedding calling him again. He'd seen several missed calls but hadn't thought it was important.

"Mr. Hale . . . this is Stanley from Black Tie Events. You rented that limo from us for your wedding."

"That's right." Brandon pressed the phone to his ear as he waited to see where this guy was going with this conversation.

"We've been trying to reach you. We wanted to let you know that our technician inspected the vehicle's flat tire. As it turns out, the tire had been slashed."

"What?" Brandon's eyebrows drew together, and he wasn't sure if he'd understood him correctly.

"That's right," Stanley said. "Whoever flattened that tire did it on purpose."

Brandon's thoughts rushed as he let that realization sink in.

———

Finley saw the surprise on Brandon's face and wondered exactly who he was talking to.

As soon as he put his phone away, she stared at him, waiting for him to explain.

He shook his head as if still trying to comprehend something. "That was the limo company. I don't even think I ever told you, but when I left the church building after the FBI arrested you, I noticed we had a flat tire on our limo. I marked it off as just more rotten luck—along with catered food for the reception going bad, the flower situation, and the rain. It just seemed like the odds weren't in our favor."

"It doesn't seem like they were, does it?"

He shifted. "The guy from the limo company said that the tire was slashed."

Finley's breath caught. "What?"

He nodded slowly, his face still tense. "I have to say, I wasn't expecting that. At that point, no one knew what you had been accused of. So I can't blame the protesters for sabotaging our limo."

Finley's thoughts raced. "Does that mean that the person who did this to me may have been on the island before I was arrested? May have even been at our wedding? May have even been in town just so they could watch all of this unfurling at me?"

Brandon's jaw tightened. "That's a possibility. But who could that even be? Who might be acting like a close friend when in reality they actually set you up? Because that seems even more dangerous than someone who's openly an enemy."

As Finley's thoughts raced, she shook her head. Almost immediately, a pulse started at her temples.

That update changed everything.

"I don't even want to imagine who could be guilty." The thought of it made Finley sick to her stomach. Someone setting her up and then watching this all unfold?

She could barely handle the realization.

She glanced around again but saw no one suspicious.

"We know we can rule out my colleagues at Blackout," Brandon said. "So who does that leave?"

"That leaves any of my coworkers who came I guess." Finley hadn't really had any of her friends there other than Amanda. But Amanda was a lawyer, and Finley couldn't see her being behind any of this for multiple reasons—including the fact that she knew nothing about technology.

"What about Ron Winslow?" Brandon asked.

"Ron? I mean, I suppose he could be a possibility, though I'd hate to think that about him."

Brandon pushed away his plate of half-eaten

food, his appetite clearly gone also. "I'm going to look into Ron to start with. I'll have my guys talk to some of the other guests at the wedding to see if they saw anything. If someone managed to slip away from the ceremony to slash that tire, there's a good chance someone may have seen this person leaving."

"At first, this news made me angry . . ." Finley admitted with a slow nod. "But now I think maybe it will help us to narrow down a new pool of suspects."

CHAPTER
THIRTY

BRANDON QUICKLY PAID for their lunch and then headed back toward the airport so they could take the helicopter to Lantern Beach.

He could clearly see that Finley was shaken by this turn of events. He only hoped this new lead might provide some answers.

The airport was a good forty-minute drive away from where they were. They could have hit one of the more commercial airports, but a smaller airport was a safer bet, given the throngs of people trying to send Finley a message.

As they headed down the road, Brandon glanced in the mirror and noticed a blue truck behind them. The vehicle had been tailing them for the past several miles, but the driver was keeping his distance.

It could simply be a coincidence, and they could

both be heading in the same direction at the same time.

But Brandon would keep an eye on the vehicle.

Three miles later, the truck was still behind them.

Brandon spontaneously turned left onto a smaller country road.

"What are you doing?" Finley asked.

He glanced in the rearview mirror again. "I just need to see if we're being followed."

She swung her head toward the back window to look. "Being followed?"

"It may not be anything, and I didn't want to concern you. But this guy has been behind us for at least fifteen minutes now, and I need to make sure that he's not up to something."

"How would anyone have found us . . . ?" Her voice drifted with fear.

"That's the question I keep asking myself also. Somehow, they must have. I suppose they could have been watching Ryan's house if they thought he could be a suspect, and they could have followed from there. But I really can't say."

"I don't like this, Brandon." Her voice trembled.

"Believe me, I don't either."

He glanced behind him and didn't see the truck.

However, he hadn't seen the vehicle pass on the street where they'd turned either.

He gripped the steering wheel harder as he headed down the road.

The GPS redirected him on his route.

They would get to the airport about fifteen minutes later this way, but it would be worth it to have some peace of mind.

Just when Brandon thought they were in the clear, he saw a vehicle appear on the road behind him.

It was the same truck.

He and Finley were definitely being followed.

He braced himself for whatever was about to happen.

————

Finley glanced over her shoulder and felt her blood go cold. "That truck is following us."

"Yes, it is." Brandon pressed the gas pedal harder to accelerate.

The narrow, two-lane road cut through green cornfields with stalks only four or five feet tall. There was little to conceal them—other than that corn, which would offer little protection.

"What do you think this guy is going to do if he catches up to us?" Finley's voice sounded strained.

"I don't plan on finding out." Brandon pressed the pedal even harder.

She glanced over her shoulder again.

It appeared the other driver also accelerated. He was gaining on them and closing the distance between them.

Finley looked back at the road ahead, and her breath caught. "Brandon . . ."

They approached an intersection with a stop sign.

It wasn't a busy area with traffic, so that wasn't Finley's worry.

No, her worry was the fact that she could see a large combine heading toward the intersection.

They were going to hit that intersection at the same time. The combine operator didn't appear to see them or to be slowing down.

"We've got to get across that road before the combine," Brandon said. "We can't afford to get stopped by it."

Her pulse pounded harder. She knew what he was saying.

But she didn't like the scenarios playing out in her head.

Scenarios that involved pain . . . not just for her but for Brandon also.

She glanced at the farm equipment again as it headed toward them.

If they managed to get past it, it would be by the skin of their teeth.

At that thought, Finley pressed her eyes shut and began to pray.

CHAPTER
THIRTY-ONE

BRANDON GLANCED AT THE COMBINE, and his lungs tightened.

This would be close.

But he could do it. He knew he could. He had no other choice.

He glanced in the rearview mirror again and saw that the truck was gaining speed much more quickly than Brandon had expected.

He didn't want to think about what that driver might do if he caught up with them.

Run them off the road? And then what?

The driver could either drive away or step out of his vehicle to finish him and Finley off for good.

Brandon wasn't going to let that happen.

He pressed the accelerator all the way to the floor.

The SUV sped forward.

The operator of the combine pressed on his

brakes. But it was too late to stop the fifteen-ton machine. He began waving out the window at Brandon, motioning for them to stop.

But Brandon couldn't do that.

Instead, he reached the intersection.

When he looked over, the combine was close enough to touch.

Brandon's lungs tightened as he anticipated the impact.

But they didn't collide.

As they moved past the intersection, he released his breath.

They'd only been a few inches from missing that equipment.

Thankfully, the driver behind him had no choice but to slam on brakes.

Now Brandon needed to get as far away as he could before that driver could catch up with him again.

———

Finley's heart was still pulsing in her ears, and she could hardly breathe.

That had been close. Too close.

She'd opened her eyes just in time to see the combine charging at them.

But Brandon had made it past.

She glanced back and saw the equipment was still

crossing the road.

The truck had to wait at the intersection.

Relief filled her.

It hadn't bought them much time. But hopefully it was enough to escape.

Brandon turned onto another road.

"That was some fancy driving back there," she murmured.

"I learned a few things as a Navy SEAL and in my short time with the CIA."

"It's a good thing you did."

It wasn't until ten minutes later that Finley finally felt herself relaxing.

She hadn't seen the truck reappear, and it seemed as if they really had lost that driver.

Praise God.

But her relief was short-lived.

Her phone rang, and she saw that it was Amanda.

Why was her friend calling again?

She put the phone to her ear. "Hey. What's going on?"

"I hate to say this, but I have more bad news."

Finley sucked in a breath. How could the news get any worse?

"What's going on?" she asked.

"I just got a notice that three of the families who lost loved ones when those Rangers were attacked have filed a civil suit against you."

"A civil suit?" She glanced at Brandon who gave her a questioning look. "What do you mean?"

"These people feel as if you are personally responsible for the death of their loved ones. So now it doesn't matter what the federal court decides. These people have decided to take you to court on their own. If they win their cases, you'll have to pay restitution to them."

"Can they do that? I haven't even been found guilty."

"Just think of OJ Simpson as a case in point. The jury acquitted him in his wife's murder, but the victims' families took him to court, and they won millions of dollars."

"Oh, Amanda . . . I didn't see this one coming."

"Neither did I. But this might not be over for a long time after all."

CHAPTER
THIRTY-TWO

BACK IN LANTERN BEACH, Brandon felt as if he had a lot that he needed to get done even though it was getting late.

The whole way here, he hadn't stopped thinking about everything that had happened.

He couldn't believe people were actually filing civil suits against Finley—as if she needed one more thing on her plate right now.

She'd gone upstairs to her apartment to change. While she did that, Brandon went downstairs to meet with Colton in his office. Colton had been overseeing the investigation on this end.

Colton looked up from his desk as Brandon walked in. He closed his laptop and rubbed his eyes as he leaned back in his chair. "Brandon . . . I heard you were back. How'd everything go?"

Brandon sat across from him and gave him a brief update, and Colton grunted with each new piece of information.

"How about you?" Brandon stared at his boss, hopeful that he had an update as well. "Were you able to look into any of the wedding guests?"

"As a matter of fact, yes." Colton crossed his arms. "Tali MacArthur happened to see a man leave the church right before the ceremony. She ran back out to her truck to get some tissues—she always cries at weddings, she said. Anyway, when she was in the parking lot, she saw a man slip out the front door and circle behind the church building."

Brandon's breath caught. "Really? Who was it? Did she recognize him?"

"It just happened to be . . . Ron Winslow."

"What?" Brandon's voice climbed with surprise. "Really? We just talked to that guy not long ago. We visited him in the office, and he's the one who escorted Finley out after the board forced her to step down for a while."

Colton shrugged. "I don't know what this Ron guy's motive could be. In fact, I had Titus put a tail on him."

"And did Ron go anywhere suspicious?" Brandon waited with anticipation for Colton's response.

Colton raised an eyebrow and shrugged again. "That's the thing. He didn't even go in to work. Titus talked to some of his coworkers, and not only did Ron not come in today, but no one's been able to reach him by phone either.

Brandon's heart raced.

Could Ron be the one behind this?

It was worth checking out.

———

Finley had considered taking a shower, but she changed her mind and simply washed her face instead.

Then she wandered downstairs to meet Brandon. She knew he'd gone to Colton's office, and she was anxious to hear an update.

Brandon's and Colton's voices drifted out into the hallway as she approached the office.

Just as she reached the doorway, she paused.

She hadn't intended on eavesdropping. But their conversation caught her ear, nonetheless.

"Unfortunately, we've had three clients decide to break their contracts," Colton said. "They said they don't want to work with us anymore."

Finley's heart pounded harder.

"What?" Brandon asked. "Is this because we're affiliated with Finley?"

"I'm not going to beat around the bush," Colton said. "It is."

"Are you concerned about what this will do for business?"

Finley didn't stick around to hear the rest. Instead, she hurried back up to her apartment.

It was just as she feared. Her arrest was affecting everyone connected to her.

She couldn't just let other people suffer because of her. It wasn't fair. She might not ever be able to salvage the remains of her life. But other people could—it wasn't too late for them.

However, she first had to cut ties with them.

Finley didn't want to be rash or impulsive. It wasn't her MO.

But if she was going to do this, she had to move quickly.

Her lungs were so tight that she could hardly breathe as she pulled out a piece of paper and began writing a note to Brandon.

With every word, she forced herself to hold her tears at bay. If she started crying right now, she might not ever stop. She knew this would be best for him.

Finley finished the letter and signed her name. Then she took off her engagement ring and placed it atop the note on the kitchen table. She quickly grabbed her bag and slipped into the hallway.

No one else was nearby.

However, there was no way she'd be able to walk off this campus without being seen.

Instead, she walked two doors down and quietly knocked on the apartment there.

A few minutes later, Amanda answered. Her friend's eyes narrowed with surprise when she saw Finley. "What's wrong?"

Finley swallowed hard before saying, "I need you to do me a big favor."

CHAPTER
THIRTY-THREE

BRANDON TRIED to put Colton's words out of his mind as he walked upstairs to meet Finley.

He wasn't going to tell her the update about Blackout's lost business. It wasn't that he wanted to keep things from her. But she had enough on her mind without worrying about the situation here.

He knew her well enough to know that's exactly what she would do. Finley would worry about the ripple effects of her arrest and blame herself when she shouldn't.

Brandon reached her room and knocked on the door. His conversation with Colton had taken longer than he anticipated.

Finley didn't answer.

Maybe she was in the shower.

He knocked again, but there was still nothing.

This time, he twisted the handle. It was unlocked.

He cracked the door open and called, "Finley?"

Still no response, and he didn't hear pounding water from a shower.

Tension began to creep up his back.

"Finley, it's me. Brandon. Are you in here?"

His worry deepened when there was no response.

Brandon tried to rein in his thoughts, to not think in worst-case scenarios. Maybe Finley stepped outside to get some fresh air.

But he'd search this apartment first just to make sure. He didn't want to overstep, but this wasn't like her.

As he glanced around the room, his gaze stopped on the paper left on the kitchen table.

When Brandon saw the ring on top of it, his heart thudded against his chest.

———

Brandon slowly lowered himself onto the kitchen chair and tried to focus on the words written on the paper.

My Dearest Brandon,

I love you so much. You're the best thing that could have happened to me. From the moment we met, I knew you were the one for me. We've been through a lot of ups and downs in the time since we've known each other, but I always prayed my path would bring me back to you.

And it did.

But I can't continue letting this lie that has been told about me also destroy your life. I love you too much to let that happen. You deserve happiness and not to be under the burden of what I'm facing. I know you're selfless and that you'd stick with me. That's just one more reason to love you.

But I can't let you do that.

I knew if I had this conversation face-to-face with you that you would convince me to stay. That's why I'm leaving this note.

I'm going to get out there and find some answers. And maybe—just maybe—if this ever clears up, we can reconnect. But I understand if you don't want that.

You deserve all the happiness in the world.

I wish I could be the one to give that to you. But life decided it wanted to take a different route for me.

Please know that I love you with all of my heart. This isn't what I want to do.

It's what I have to do.
With all my love,
Finley

Warm tears pricked his eyes. It was just as he feared—Finley was trying to be selfless. To protect him.

And now she was gone.

But Brandon knew she still loved him, and he wanted nothing more than to walk through this trial with her.

He picked up her ring and slid it into his wallet.

Things between them weren't going to end like this.

He would find Finley and bring her back—if it was the last thing he did.

Quickly, he hit her phone number on his cell.

But her phone didn't even ring.

She'd either turned it off or destroyed it, hadn't she?

He frowned. That's what he would have told her to do, so it was hard to even be upset.

With his keys in his hands, he started toward the door. Lantern Beach wasn't a big island, and the ferry ran on a schedule. If Finley wanted to get away from here, that's most likely the route she'd take.

The helicopter that had been here earlier was now gone, otherwise he would get up in the air for an aerial view of the island.

Since that wasn't an option, Brandon climbed into his SUV, determined to find her.

CHAPTER
THIRTY-FOUR

FINLEY CROUCHED under a blanket in the back seat as Amanda left Blackout Headquarters. The guard waved them through while the crowd outside continued to chant.

Amanda had insisted on coming with her, had seemed to understand her need to get away. Finley had told Amanda she didn't have to—that Finley only wanted to borrow her car—but Amanda hadn't listened. She'd contended that being a reviled attorney would only be good for business and that was how criminal law worked.

Somehow, her explanation made sense.

Once they were past the protestors, Finley threw the blanket off and sat up, drawing in the cooler air. "Is it safe?"

"It appears so. But wear those sunglasses and the hat, just in case."

Finley slid them on as she climbed into the front seat and stared out the window.

The protestors—the ones who so desperately wanted to make her pay—were behind them now.

However, Finley knew there was no way she'd get out of this situation unscathed.

She hoped that maybe Brandon would, at least.

"So where are we going?" Amanda glanced at her.

"I'm not really sure." Finley crossed her arms and frowned. She hadn't thought things through that much yet. "I guess we need to get off the island first. It's only a matter of time before Brandon discovers I'm gone, and I know he'll come after me."

"It's kind of sweet, really." A sad smile crossed Amanda's lips.

A lump formed in Finley's throat. "It is. But . . . our relationship just can't happen now, you know?"

"I do. This has been a lot. I'm surprised Brandon stuck by you like he has."

Finley did a double take at her friend, unsure if she'd heard Amanda correctly. "Why do you say that?"

Amanda shrugged as if the conversation were casual. "It's not because I don't think he's a good guy. Don't get me wrong. But who wants to attach themselves to this kind of headache? It's like being in a sinking boat, and you have a chance to put on a life preserver and jump ship. Most people wouldn't want to stick around."

Defensiveness rose in her. "Brandon's not that type of man."

"I know you don't want to hear that. And maybe I'm wrong. But I've seen some really amazing people buckle under pressure."

Finley's chest tightened. She didn't like the sound of that. Amanda clearly didn't know Brandon like Finley did.

Yet, despite that, for some reason, the conversation bothered her.

Why would Amanda want to put doubts in her head at a time like this?

Instead of dwelling on it, Finley stared out the window as she and Amanda drove across the island.

Finally, the ferry terminal came into view. The boat already appeared full, and one of the crew members stood beside the gate as if about to close it.

If they missed this ferry . . . then Brandon would definitely find her. The ferry only ran every three hours.

"No!" Finley muttered. "Do you think it's too late?"

"Let's find out." Amanda eased her car up to the entrance and put down her window. "Any chance we can make this?"

"We just loaded the last car."

"It's kind of an emergency. My friend is facing a

family emergency and has to get to the hospital up in Norfolk. Please . . . it's urgent."

The worker stared at her a moment before nodding. "Fine. We have space for one more, so get on. But be quick about it."

Relief washed through her as Amanda pulled onto the boat and eased close behind the vehicle in front of her.

Just as Amanda put her car in Park, the gates closed, and the ferry worker signaled the captain on the top deck.

Finley released the breath she'd been holding.

Thanks to Amanda, it looked like the two of them might just get off of this island in time.

———

As Brandon hopped into his car and took off down the road, he called Cassidy and told her about Finley. Maybe Cassidy could help him locate Finley before she did something foolish.

"I'm sorry to hear she left," Cassidy's voice came through his speaker.

Something about the way she said those words didn't sound hopeful. "Can you put a BOLO out for her?"

"I wish I could, Brandon. But it's not a crime to leave. I can't spend my resources on that. She's an adult. If Finley wants to leave, then you have to let her. There's nothing illegal about it."

Despite the fact that Brandon understood Cassidy's words, his jaw hardened. "She's going to get herself killed."

"I understand the situation." Cassidy softened her voice. "And I'm sorry. I really am. But there's nothing I can do."

Brandon's back muscles knit together so tightly that an ache formed between his shoulders. He knew what Cassidy said was true—but he didn't like it.

"If you see her, could you let me know, at least?" he finally asked.

"I can do that."

At least, it was *something*.

Brandon headed toward the ferry terminal—the most logical place Finley would go.

As he drove down the road, he kept his eyes peeled and looked for any signs of her.

It felt like it took hours to reach the docks, when in reality it was probably twenty minutes.

Just as Brandon drove up, the ferry pulled away.

He climbed out of his SUV to take a better look.

When he did, he saw Finley. She stood at the back of the boat, a melancholy look on her face as she offered him a halfhearted wave.

Almost as if it was her final goodbye.

A lump formed in his throat at the sight of her . . . and at how final this moment felt.

CHAPTER
THIRTY-FIVE

ANOTHER TEAR TRICKLED down Finley's cheek as Brandon as well as Lantern Beach disappeared from sight.

The briny scent of the Pamlico Sound mixed with her salty tears as water splashed from the back of the boat and covered her face. Seagulls swooped around her, diving with the breeze and begging for any crumbs naïve passengers might offer them.

Finley had been trying hard to keep her emotions under control. But it was difficult.

Especially when she saw the expression on Brandon's face.

He looked heartbroken.

She should have stayed inside Amanda's car. She shouldn't have gotten out to take one last look at the island.

But another part of her hadn't been able to stop herself.

Who knew when she'd see Brandon again? He'd probably try to look for her, but Finley would do her best to remain hidden.

He needed to let her go.

It was the only thing that made sense. If he wasn't so loyal, he'd see that too.

But he'd never leave her willingly. So it was up to her to make things right.

"I'm sorry, Finley. I know how difficult this must be." Amanda stared out at the water as the distance between the ferry and land grew greater.

Other passengers had climbed out of their vehicles to watch the journey too. Someone beside them exclaimed that they'd spotted dolphins playing in the boat's wake.

Everything seemed so normal around her.

Except nothing was normal for her.

"We should probably get back in the car," Amanda told her quietly. "We don't want anyone to recognize you."

Finley knew her friend was right.

She slipped back into her seat and cracked the window to get some air. Then she slunk down low so no one would give her another glance.

She hoped. The last thing she needed was for people to catch wind of who she was. Facing protestors while on the ferry would be horrific.

"Thank you for being here for me." She glanced at Amanda.

"Of course. I'll always be here for you, just like you were there for me after Jerry passed." Her voice cracked.

Finley reached over and squeezed her arm, knowing how painful his death had been. Grief . . . it could be a horrible thing to contend with. Finley had dealt with it both when her mother died and then later her father. She hadn't even felt like herself.

"At least, you still have Brandon." Amanda offered a sympathetic shrug. "He's still . . . alive, right?"

Finley wasn't sure how to respond to that. Finally, she said, "He is. But he deserves much better than all of this. So much better."

"From what you've told me, that's not the way he thinks."

Finley frowned. "Exactly. And that's the problem."

———

There was no way Brandon would simply go back to Blackout and sit there.

But he knew the next ferry wouldn't leave for a few hours, so he headed back to Blackout. He needed to pack a bag since he wasn't sure how long he'd be gone once he got off this island.

After he threw some things together, he stopped by Colton's office and gave him the update.

Colton paced to the window and peered out at the protestors still there. "Why do you think Finley took off? Did something happen?"

"Part of me wonders if she overheard some of our conversation. You know she's pretty selfless. I don't think she likes the strain she's been putting us under. She feels guilty about it."

Colton frowned and rubbed his jaw. "I'm sorry to hear that. We're willing to do whatever it takes to help her. That still stands."

"I know, and I appreciate that."

Colton turned away from the window and back toward Brandon. "What are you going to try to do?"

Determination hardened inside him. "I'm going to find her. And I'm going to find the person who set her up. I'm going to start with Ron."

"So you're going to Raleigh?"

"It seems as good a place as any to start." Brandon offered a tight nod. "Maybe he'll be able to give me some answers. In the meantime, Finley's not answering her phone, so I can't even get in touch with her."

"Just give her time. Do you want me to go with you? Or one of the other guys?"

Brandon shook his head. He'd already thought that much through. "This is something I need to do on my own. But if I need backup or if I get myself into a bind, I'll let you know."

"You do that. Be safe."

With another nod at his friend, Brandon left.

He had to find some answers.

He had no time to waste.

CHAPTER
THIRTY-SIX

TWO HOURS after Finley and Amanda got off the ferry, they pulled up to a small house in the middle of the swampy landscape of coastal North Carolina.

From what Amanda had told her, the hunting cabin belonged to one of Amanda's colleagues at the law firm, and he'd said she could use it.

As they'd driven here, Finley hadn't seen any other houses or signs of life for at least twenty miles.

This place was surrounded by trees, patches of swampy water, and deep ditches edged with marsh grass.

"It's not exactly paradise, but it will do," Amanda muttered as she stared at the clapboard cabin in front of them. "Just as a matter of fair warning, there are bears and alligators out here."

"Alligators?"

She nodded. "Believe it or not, yes. I've seen them

myself. Oh, and there's no Wi-Fi, cell service, or internet."

Finley supposed no Wi-Fi was a good thing, considering the circumstances.

Yet at the same time it made her feel slightly uncomfortable. Not that she had a cell phone with her. But she and Amanda were definitely cut off from the rest of the world in this secluded cabin.

"I know being cut off from the web sounds like a bummer, but it's probably a blessing in disguise," Amanda added. "No one can trace us this way."

That was true. This definitely seemed like a place Brandon wouldn't find them.

Finley's gut still twisted into knots at the thought of Brandon and how he must be feeling right now.

But she kept reminding herself that all this was for the best.

Maybe in the meantime she could figure out who'd set her up.

It was the only acceptable resolution she could think of.

She stepped inside the rustic building. The humidity from outside had taken claim inside this place too.

Amanda seemed to read her thoughts.

"No AC," she muttered, dropping her bag near the door. "We'll use ceiling fans instead. We can't open the windows. Too many bugs—and there are tears in the screens."

"I'm sure it will be fine." Finley resisted the urge to fan her face.

Beggars couldn't be choosers. Wasn't that how the saying went?

She glanced around and noted the dark paneled walls and furniture. Numerous animal heads hung above the couch and fireplace, and the furnishings were outdated.

Not exactly her dream vacation home. But that was okay—she wouldn't complain.

"There are two bedrooms, one for each of us," Amanda explained. "Why don't you take the one in the back?"

"That sounds good." Finley took her things to her room, and several minutes later, she and Amanda met back in the tiny kitchen.

Amanda found some chicken and rice soup that hadn't expired and began heating it on the stove. They also found some crackers and bottled water.

"So what's our next plan of action?" Finley asked as she sat at the breakfast bar watching Amanda cook.

"That's up to you to decide what you want to do."

"I mean . . . as far as legal issues."

"Oh, right." Amanda stirred the steaming soup and frowned. "I'm hoping we're going to find a decent lead. Right now, the fact that the timelines don't add up will work in our favor. I'm just not sure that will be enough."

"I'm not either." Finley licked her lips and considered whether or not she should share with Amanda the fact she'd sent that fake party invitation link out to her top three suspects.

She knew Amanda wouldn't be happy with her.

For now, Finley would wait, she decided. Maybe later she'd share that information—but only if it seemed necessary. Though Amanda was her lawyer, and they had attorney-client confidentiality, it was best if her friend didn't know.

A few minutes later, Amanda ladled some soup into two bowls. The savory aroma of chicken broth filled Finley's nostrils and brought a temporary moment of comfort.

But the comfort didn't last long.

Because a moment later, a creak sounded on the rickety porch.

Finley's back muscles pinched.

Had someone found them here?

———

Brandon drove to Raleigh. It was getting late, but he had no time to lose.

For that reason, he went straight to Ron's house and rang the doorbell. When the man didn't answer,

Brandon walked around the perimeter of the place and peered in his windows.

Just as Titus had said, Ron wasn't there.

Had the man been taken? Or had he disappeared because he was guilty?

There had to be a way to figure out where he'd gone.

As Brandon headed back to his car, a man walking a golden retriever paused on the sidewalk. "You looking for Ron?"

Brandon contemplated the best response. "I am. Do you happen to know where I could find him? I'm supposed to take him out to celebrate his promotion at work."

"A promotion at work? That sounds like Ron. I can't tell you for sure where he went, but when he left here this morning, I saw he had some camping gear with him. He must have forgotten his plans with you."

"I should have probably reminded him." Brandon shrugged, trying to appear easygoing. "It is beautiful weather to go camping. I can't blame him for that."

"Me neither."

"I wonder if he headed to the mountains." Brandon was fishing for information.

"Maybe. But I figured he probably went out to Holly Springs. You know how he likes to stay at the campground there whenever he has a chance."

Holly Springs? Brandon stored that name away. "I

think I did hear him mention something about wanting to go there."

The man's dog tugged at his leash, and he waved. "Anyway, have a good evening! Sally is losing her patience."

"I'll try to catch him later." Brandon offered the friendly neighbor a wave as the man continued by with the dog. "Thank you!"

His smile slipped as soon as the neighbor turned from him.

He needed to go to Ron's favorite campground and see if he could find him there.

CHAPTER
THIRTY-SEVEN

"DID YOU HEAR THAT TOO?" Finley's gaze shot to Amanda.

"I did." Amanda set down the spoon near the pot of soup and stiffened. "What do you think it was?"

"Could someone have followed us?" Finley's voice sounded scratchy as she said the words.

"I don't see how. I kept my eye on the road. And you didn't bring your phone, right?"

"No, I took the battery out, and I left it at the apartment so I couldn't be traced."

"Then no one should know that we're here, no one except the guy who owns this place." Amanda frowned as she stared at the front of the house where the sound had come from.

"Can you trust him?"

"Yes, I've known him since I joined the firm."

A creak sounded on the porch again.

Finley's spine tightened.

Amanda's gaze latched onto Finley's. "What are we going to do?"

Her gaze scanned the room and stopped on a butcher block full of knives.

Wasting no more time, Finley strode across the room and grabbed one. She gripped the six-inch blade tightly in her hand and then turned toward the front door.

"You're not thinking about going out there, are you?" Amanda practically gasped as she asked the question.

"What else are we going to do? Just sit in here and wait for them to attack?"

"Finley . . . you've got to think this through."

"There's nothing else to think about. Besides, I want to see the person who's done this to me. I'm so tired of hiding."

As she strode toward the door, Amanda whispered, "Finley . . . I hope you know what you're doing."

Finley knew she might regret this burst of bravado she felt. But another part of her was tired of living in fear.

She wanted answers.

If this person was going to kill her, then he would either kill her by breaking into the house or kill her when she stepped out.

The time and place really made little difference.

When she reached the door, another moment of doubt flashed through her.

Fear nearly overtook her.

But she pushed through it.

Finley gripped the door handle and flung the door open. She stretched her arm out, pushing the knife forward as a blast of humid air nearly attacked her.

However, she needed to let whoever was out here know she meant business.

She braced herself for whatever she was about to find.

———

By the time Brandon pulled into the campground, it was already dark outside.

The good news was the place wasn't that large. If Ron was here, Brandon should be able to find him.

Brandon paid for a site at the front gate then parked at his assigned spot.

He took out his flashlight and began walking along the gravel drive of the campground.

Each site was wooded and secluded, which was probably why Ron liked it here.

Several people staying here had already started campfires and sat around the flames, talking and laughing, singing, and making s'mores.

The sounds and the smells were so lighthearted

and fun that Brandon's heart panged with a moment of loss.

What he wouldn't give to be able to kick back and have some fun.

But right now, he could only think about Finley. She had to be his main focus.

The attendant had given him a map of this place when he'd paid, and Brandon knew he needed to walk at least a mile in order to pass by all the sites. There was only one road through the campground, and it formed a loop from start to finish.

Brandon knew that Ron drove a white Land Rover.

That was what he would look for.

As he paced the road, his mind wandered to Finley again. The two of them had talked about going camping sometime. She'd never been before, which Brandon found unbelievable. He'd told her he needed to change that. He'd been trying to figure out plans to go to the mountains in the fall so they could camp and watch the leaves change.

Now it looked like they may not ever get that chance.

Why did Finley have to be so strong-willed and stubborn?

On the other hand, that was what Brandon loved about her. Her vivacity and determination.

However, that same vivacity had led to her leaving today.

Brandon almost reached the halfway point on the loop when his flashlight beam hit a car in the distance.

A Land Rover.

This must be Ron's campsite.

Brandon felt a surge of adrenaline rush through him as he cut his light and walked closer, determined to figure out what this man was hiding.

CHAPTER
THIRTY-EIGHT

FINLEY HELD her breath as she braced herself for an attack.

Instead, she saw a deer scampering toward the woods.

She nearly laughed with relief.

All of this drama had been because of a deer?

She lowered the knife in her hands and shook her head.

Just to be certain, she glanced around one more time. She didn't want to let down her guard too easily.

However, she saw no signs that anyone was close.

Only trees and swampland stared back.

"Finley?" Amanda's trembling voice sounded behind her.

She stepped back inside and turned to her friend. "It was nothing. Just a deer."

Amanda nearly went limp as she leaned against the kitchen counter. "I'm so glad. I had a ton of worst-case scenarios going through my head."

Finley paced back over toward the counter and left the knife there before sliding onto a barstool. "Me too."

Amanda's gaze met hers. "You were so brave. And I froze."

"We never know how we're going to react in these situations, do we?"

Amanda shook her head. "No, we don't. But we should be safe here. No one should be able to find us."

"That's a relief," Finley nodded at the soup. "I don't know about you, but I'm ready to eat."

She needed something to distract herself from everything.

She'd already lost so much.

But so much more was on the line.

Hiding out here would only work for a little while.

But not very long. Because Finley was determined to find answers.

And she hoped Amanda would help her.

———

Just as Brandon neared the campsite, the tent opened, and a man stepped out. As he did, Brandon turned the flashlight on, and the beam hit the man's face.

Ron Winslow.

The man looked like a deer caught in headlights.

He didn't look professional in his jeans and black T-shirt. In fact, he was nearly unrecognizable out of his business suit.

As soon as Ron snapped out of his stupor, he turned to run.

"I wouldn't do that," Brandon said.

Ron froze, his hands in the air. Sweat covered his skin, and his breaths came fast and shallow. "I don't want any trouble."

"I don't want trouble either. Just answers." Brandon stepped closer and held the light to his own face so Ron would know who he was. "I'm not going to hurt you."

"Brandon?"

"It's me." He paused in front of him. "We have a lot of people looking for you."

Ron swallowed hard and rubbed his throat. "I know. I didn't want to hide. But I had no choice."

Brandon would reserve his judgment on that. "I need you to tell me what's going on."

Ron glanced around as if to see if Brandon had brought anyone else with him. The man was clearly spooked.

"I'm alone. We need to talk." Brandon nodded to a picnic table close to the campfire pit.

Ron slowly walked toward it and sat down stiffly on one of the benches. Brandon sat a couple of feet away and angled himself toward the man, just in case he tried anything.

Brandon decided to get right to the point. "What happened?"

"After I got home last night, two guys broke in."

"Why?"

Ron shook his head, his eyes glazed. "I'm not sure. I didn't stick around long enough to find out."

"What happened?"

"I ran into a safe room in my house. I don't think they knew I was there."

"You have any idea why they showed up?"

"The only thing I can figure is that it was because one of our tech guys found evidence that someone had been poking around in our software at Embolden. Someone hacked into our program and gave information to the Chinese. Just for the record, the IP address did not trace back to Finley."

Brandon's heart beat harder. "Who did you trace it back to?"

"I was trying to figure that out when those men broke in. But I'd already sent some of the evidence that proves this isn't Finley to the FBI, even before the break-in. I thought it was only right to do so."

"Did you tell Finley?"

Ron shook his head. "Not yet. I didn't want to get her hopes up."

"Can you still figure out who may have done this?" Brandon's eyes bore into Ron as he waited for his answer.

"I brought my laptop. I'm trying."

"Good. Keep doing that." Brandon shifted as his thoughts churned. "Can you describe either of the men who came to your house?"

"I watched them on the security camera. I have a monitor set up in my safe room. Once they were inside, they pulled off their masks—they probably didn't think I had cameras. They were in their late twenties or early thirties. One of them has a scar across his right cheek."

"What kind of scar?"

"It looked like a lightning bolt."

Brandon squinted as he tried to picture that. "A lightning bolt? That's pretty distinctive."

"The two of them seemed like they knew what they were doing, like they'd done it before."

Brandon stored that fact away. "Thank you. I'll look into them. Can you send me video of the men?"

"I'll see if I can pull it up. It might take a while. Internet service isn't reliable out here."

"That would be great."

Ron's fearful gaze jerked toward Brandon. "Are you going to report me?"

"I'm not going to report you because it doesn't

sound like you've done anything wrong. But I'd watch your back if I were you. These guys might track you down here like I did."

"I'll be careful." Ron's voice wavered. "I'm really sorry this happened to Finley. I never thought she was guilty. But I just had to follow the company's protocol."

"I get it." Brandon stood. "If what you told me is true, you should lie low."

"I plan on it."

"And if you hear anything else, please let me know." Brandon handed him a business card. "You're not the only one in danger right now. The faster you can trace the IP address to a specific person, the sooner everyone will be safe."

"Understood."

"And I'll need the name of the tech who helped you discover someone hacked into the software at Embolden. He could be in danger."

Ron rattled off the man's name.

With that, Brandon turned the flashlight on and started back down the road toward his SUV.

CHAPTER
THIRTY-NINE

AS SOON AS Brandon was back in his SUV, he called Colton.

"I was just about to call you," Colton said.

"What's going on?" He didn't like the sound of his friend's voice.

"FBI Agent Bills just showed up here. Bills said he wants to talk to Finley."

"And . . ." Brandon wasn't sure where Colton was going with this.

"He said they got an anonymous tip that she was in South Carolina."

His breath caught. "South Carolina? Why would she go there? She knows better."

"I don't know. Maybe it's all a ruse. That's what I'm hoping, at least."

"You and me both." Brandon didn't like the sinking feeling in his gut.

"I'm assuming that's not why you called," Colton said.

Brandon's mind snapped back to his conversation with Ron—for now. "I need you to do me a favor. Can you look through the crime databases and see if you can find anyone with a lightning bolt scar across his right cheek? It sounds unique."

"Sure thing. I'll see what I can find out. But it might take me a few minutes. I'm going to put you on hold while I check."

"Sounds good." Brandon leaned back in his seat, his thoughts racing through what Ron had told him.

Had someone discovered that Ron and his tech guy had uncovered that data leak? If this person wanted to frame Finley, and if Ron had found evidence to clear her, then maybe the culprit wanted to silence Ron and the tech guy permanently.

It seemed extreme.

But everything this person had done had been extreme.

Finally, Colton came back on the phone. "I think I found him. A guy named Clyde Smith was released from prison about three months ago. He has a scar like that."

"What was he in for?"

"He hacked into the FBI's database and sold sensitive information on several agents to members of the cartel. He went to prison for five years."

Brandon's breath caught as anticipation rose

inside him. "Okay . . . cyber security issues would fit with what happened with Finley. But what connection does this guy have with her?"

Colton read out a few more facts about the case before pausing.

"What's wrong?" Brandon instantly sensed his friend had discovered something.

"This can't be a coincidence," Colton muttered. "But it says that the man's defense attorney was . . . none other than Amanda Higgins."

"Amanda Higgins?" Brandon's voice rose as he said the woman's name.

Had Finley's friend been somehow involved in this the whole time?

Brandon's heart raced faster.

Finley was with Amanda right now.

A surge of panic flooded through him.

He had to figure out a way to find Finley before it was too late.

————

Finley finished her soup and washed the dishes. Then she and Amanda went to sit on the couch.

They hadn't talked about the case over dinner. Amanda had reminisced about Jerry instead and talked about how different life was without him.

The couple had truly seemed as if they were made for each other.

But now Finley hoped they might be able to talk about the case.

As they sat there wearing shorts and T-shirts, Finley was reminded of their old study sessions back in high school. Back then, they'd eaten junk to stay awake, a luxury they could no longer afford. But Hot Fries and Skittles had been their junk food of choice.

Those days seemed so worry-free compared to now.

"This gets even better." Amanda moved the curtain aside and peered outside. "It's a full moon tonight. We both know what that means."

"That people get a little crazier than usual?"

"People and animals."

Finley frowned. The thought didn't make her feel any better. "Did you ever find out from the prosecutor what this new evidence is that came to light?" Finley pulled her knees to her chest as she waited for her friend's answer.

Amanda tucked her legs beneath her. "They were supposed to get back with me about that. I suppose I could check my emails to see if they've sent me anything. But, like I told you earlier, there's no Wi-Fi here."

"There's none at all? I know sometimes in places like this you might pick up on a signal on occasion."

"It's worth checking." Amanda grabbed her computer, hit a few keys, and then frowned. "Nope. There's nothing. Maybe in the morning I can drive out to the store to pick up some things, and I'll check while I'm there."

Finley nodded, disappointed that she would have to wait longer. But it didn't appear she had much choice.

"What am I going to do, Amanda?" Finley glanced at her friend and frowned.

Amanda hit a few more keys on her laptop before closing the screen. "We'll figure out something. I'm going to fight for you with everything I've got. I promise you that."

Finley knew her friend was one of the best attorneys out there, and she trusted Amanda's abilities.

But so much was on the line right now.

"What do we do now?" Finley asked. "I need something more concrete than that."

Amanda pulled her curly hair back into a messy bun atop her head. "I suppose we wait to see what this new evidence is. But I'm looking into the timeline of all this, just like you suggested. We should be able to prove you weren't online setting up this new bank account when everything went down."

Finley wanted to feel relief, but she didn't. "The FBI needs to see where the documents sent to the bank originated from. They should be able to track that down. Better yet, *we* should track it down because I don't trust anything the FBI is doing right now."

"You and me both." Amanda let out a sigh before

squeezing Finley's hand. "We're going to get you through this, my friend. We're going to get you through this."

She was grateful for her friend.

Finley leaned back and sighed.

When she opened her eyes again, something beneath the end table caught her eye.

A phone book.

"Is there a phone here?" Finley asked. It would be good to know . . . just in case.

It wasn't that she was planning on calling anyone.

Amanda frowned. "Not that I know about. Maybe there was a phone here at one time. I'm pretty sure there's not one anymore."

Finley squinted as she stared at the old, dusty book. That's when she noticed the small detail that had been begging for her attention.

The words "South Carolina" jumped out from the front of the book.

South Carolina? Was that where they were?

Because Finley wasn't supposed to leave North Carolina. It would break the terms of her bond and land her behind bars.

She glanced at her friend as questions rushed through her mind.

CHAPTER
FORTY

"AMANDA, why does that say South Carolina?" Finley's voice trembled as she tried to set her mind at ease.

"What?" Amanda's eyebrows shoved together. "What are you talking about?"

She grabbed the phone book and showed her friend. "This?"

Amanda's eyes widened. "We're not in South Carolina—although we're close. Maybe that's why they have it. Besides, look at the date. It's from ten years ago. Probably because when my colleague used to come here all the time, it was worth it to have a landline."

Finley let out a breath. She supposed that explanation made sense. After all, her friend and lawyer wouldn't do something to purposefully get her in trouble.

The stress of the situation just had her on edge.

She rose from her seat.

"I'm going to head to bed." Finley decided to turn in early. She was exhausted, and maybe some sleep would do her good.

She glanced at her friend and saw that Amanda looked exhausted also. Dark circles hung beneath her eyes, and she kept running a hand over her face as if trying to stay awake.

"I hope you can get some sleep," Amanda said before yawning.

"Me too. Are you going to be up much later?"

"I'll probably stay up another thirty minutes to unwind. Get yourself some rest."

Finley slipped into the bedroom and sat on her lumpy bed. But her mind was racing too fast for her to rest. Eventually, she forced herself to lie down. But every time she closed her eyes, Brandon's expression when he'd watched her leave the island filled her mind.

She could hardly live with what she'd done. Yet she had no other choice right now.

Finally, after tossing and turning for what felt like hours, Finley threw the dusty covers off and stood. The floor had several areas where the wood had splintered so she slipped on some loafers. The air was chilly, so she also tugged on an oversized cardigan.

Then she silently crept from her room, careful not to awaken Amanda.

She walked into the dark living room, almost taken back by the quiet. There was no steady hum of traffic nearby. No sirens from emergency vehicles.

She wasn't used to places this isolated.

She knew she shouldn't, but she walked toward the window and nudged the curtain out of the way. She peered at the darkness outside but didn't see anything suspicious.

Maybe they truly were safe here. For a while, at least.

Finley started toward the kitchen to get some water when she heard a buzzing noise.

She glanced around, looking for the source of the sound.

Her gaze stopped on Amanda's phone. She'd left it on the end table.

Out of curiosity, Finley paced toward it. As she lifted it, the screen lit, and she squinted when she saw Amanda had a text message there.

A text message? She thought they didn't have service here.

Why would her friend have lied to her? Or was service just spotty?

That could be a possibility. In fact, it was the only thing that made sense.

Even though Finley knew she shouldn't, she glanced at the message.

Her blood went cold as the words came into focus.

> We did what you asked. But the guy was long gone. Our hands are tied. Hopefully, you have the asset.
> Because we're done with our end of the bargain.

The asset?

Finley's breath caught.

Wait . . . was *Finley* the asset?

Was Amanda the antagonist trying to destroy her?

Finley remembered the fact that the person behind this had been at her wedding.

If her instincts were right, that person had also been inside the estate where Finley had stayed right after she was released on bail.

And someone seemed to be tracking her every move, though she'd never figured out how.

Could that be . . . Amanda?

Her heart beat harder.

At once, Finley knew she needed to get away from here.

What if Amanda had come back to Lantern Beach —but not just out of the goodness of her heart? What if none of this had been in an effort to help Finley . . . but if Amanda had wanted to frame her instead?

Finley didn't want to believe her friend could be

behind this, but the evidence seemed pretty clear right now.

But how would she get away? She was in the middle of nowhere without her own vehicle.

She glanced around, hoping her friend had left her car keys somewhere.

But they were nowhere to be found.

They must be with Amanda in her bedroom. But Finley couldn't risk sneaking in there to get them.

She would have to leave on foot, which could prove challenging since she was surrounded by swamps.

Still, if Finley could get down the long driveway and make it to the next major road, then maybe she'd eventually find some help. She could stay along the edge of the woods when possible so if Amanda did come after her, her so-called friend wouldn't be able to spot her.

It was Finley's only chance right now.

And if she was going to run, she had no time to waste.

As she stepped outside, she gripped Amanda's phone. Could she guess her friend's code and call Brandon for help?

It was worth a try.

But she was going to keep moving as she did.

———

As Brandon raced back toward Lantern Beach, his thoughts churned.

Amanda was in on this, wasn't she?

Now Amanda and Finley were together. Alone. At an unknown location.

Where could they have gone? That was what he didn't know. He had no way of tracing them.

That meant he had no way of helping Finley.

And that wasn't okay.

He had to think of something. Accepting that there were no solutions was *not* an option right now.

His thoughts continued to churn inside him. He'd already sent the local police to check on the tech guy Ron had mentioned. The man had taken a vacation to the Smoky Mountains and appeared to be okay.

Then Brandon's phone rang.

His breath caught when he saw Amanda's number pop up on the screen.

Why would Amanda be calling him?

He hit the button to answer. "Amanda?"

There was no response, just the sound of something rustling in the background.

What was going on?

"Amanda?" he called again.

Again, there was no answer.

Then the line went dead.

Something was wrong. Brandon was certain of it.

If Amanda was with Finley, and if Amanda had

her phone . . . maybe he could trace where they'd gone.

Brandon quickly called Colton and asked him to run Amanda's number and see if he could ping a location.

His friend promised to do just that.

In the meantime, Brandon continued back toward Lantern Beach.

He prayed he was heading in the right direction.

CHAPTER
FORTY-ONE

"WHAT ARE YOU DOING OUT HERE?"

Finley was about to step off the porch when she heard Amanda's voice behind her.

She twirled around and saw Amanda standing in the open doorway. She'd pulled on some joggers and a dark, hooded sweatshirt. Her hair was still in that same messy bun.

Finley drew in a deep breath and carefully slid the phone into her pocket. A couple more seconds and she could have told Brandon what was happening. She could have asked him for help.

She'd figured out Amanda's security code on the third try.

It was Jerry's birthday.

"Just getting some fresh air." Finley's best chance now was to act like everything was normal.

But she could hear Brandon's voice on the phone, saying Amanda's name.

Finley quickly pressed a side button to silence the phone, praying Amanda hadn't heard anything.

"Don't you know there are bears and alligators out here? Yes, alligators. People don't believe we have them in North Carolina, but we do." Amanda tilted her head, not bothering to hide her annoyance.

"I know, and I'm keeping my eyes open. I just can't sleep, and the fresh air feels good."

Amanda eyed her another moment as if she didn't believe her words. Then she nodded toward the door. "I think it's better if you come back inside."

Taken aback by Amanda's curt tone, Finley bristled. "I will. Just give me a minute."

The moonlight hit Amanda's face, and for some reason, her eyes seemed to be bulging in a way that almost made her look . . . crazy.

The next instant, Amanda reached into the pocket of her hoodie and withdrew . . . a gun. "You don't understand. I said, 'get back inside.'"

Finley's eyes widened. Even though she'd suspected her friend might be behind this, part of her still hoped she was wrong. Still hoped that maybe her friend was innocent in this, and that Finley had misunderstood the meaning of the text message she'd intercepted.

"Amanda . . ." Finley stared at her friend, her voice wavering. "Why do you have a gun?"

"Don't act like you don't know. I can see it written all over your face. Now get back inside. Don't make me pull this trigger." Her nostrils flared, and her muscles appeared tight enough to snap.

"Why are you doing this?" Finley still didn't move.

"You really don't know?"

"I have no idea."

Amanda practically sneered, her front lip slightly jerking up as her nostrils flared. "It's all your fault that Jerry died. I don't know how you could do this to me."

"My fault?" The breath left Finley's lungs. "Why in the world would it be my fault?"

"You're the reason he killed himself!"

Finley shook her head, still unable to process why her friend might say this. "I hardly ever talked to Jerry, except when we all went to dinner together. I have no idea how I could possibly be the reason."

"He heard you talking about some company— Smart Intelligence that was hoping to change the world as we know it."

"Okay . . ."

"And he jumped onboard and invested everything in it. All our savings."

"What? Why would he do that? I never recommended that. I was simply talking about the company."

"He thought everything you said was gold. He

didn't even tell me what he was going to do. Then we lost it all."

"I'm sorry, Amanda. But I had nothing to do with this."

"Yes, you did!" Her voice rose. "Why can't you see it? You took away the love of my life and ruined my future. Now I'm going to ruin you!"

"So you set me up as a traitor?"

She smirked. "That's right. I wanted to make sure the happiest day of your life was ruined. I couldn't have asked for better timing."

"Amanda . . ." Finley knew that it didn't matter what she said to her friend. Nothing would get through to her.

Amanda had lost her mind . . .

As if to confirm that thought, Amanda's eyes narrowed, and she muttered, "Now get inside before I put a bullet in you."

———

Brandon's apprehension continued to grow as he drove on the back roads of North Carolina toward the coast.

Finally, Colton called back. "Good news. I have a location."

He let out the breath he'd been holding. That *was* good news. "Okay. Can you send it to me?"

"I'll do that right now. It's about two hours from

Lantern Beach right over the South Carolina line. It may be a hunting cabin."

"I'm heading there now. I'm going to need backup."

"I'm already on it."

Brandon got the text message on the screen of his SUV and tapped it. It said he was thirty minutes away.

He only prayed he could get there in time. And get there without triggering Amanda.

If she wasn't already triggered.

Based on the fact Brandon had gotten that phone call, he had to believe something was wrong.

He ended his call with Colton and sped down the road.

Why in the world would Amanda do this to Finley? What sense did it even make?

Brandon knew that Amanda's husband had taken his own life not long ago. Did that have something to do with this? Had Amanda started to lose her mind after that happened?

He'd have to do some more research.

But not right now. Right now, the important thing was keeping Finley safe.

He had to somehow convince her that, when this was all over, it didn't matter if being with her made his life more complicated. He'd do anything for her. *Anything.*

He'd walk through the fire with her rather than take the easy route alone any day.

He pressed the accelerator harder as he sped toward that location.

And he prayed for the best.

CHAPTER
FORTY-TWO

FINLEY CONTINUED to stare at Amanda. No way was she going back inside with the woman she'd been friends with for so long. If she did, Finley would end up dead. She felt certain of it.

Had their friendship been a lie all these years? Or had it soured when Amanda lost her husband?

She'd figure that out later.

Right now, she needed to concentrate on survival.

Finley took a step back. "Let's talk this through."

"There's nothing to talk through," Amanda snapped as she turned to open the door. "Now get inside!"

Finley made an executive decision.

Before Amanda could fully pivot to face her again, Finley darted toward the woods.

As her feet dug into the ground a bullet ripped through the air.

Finley held her breath, waiting to feel pain.

But she didn't.

She hadn't been hit.

She didn't think so, at least.

Her adrenaline was so high that there was a possibility she couldn't feel any pain.

"Come back here!" Amanda shouted.

Then Finley heard footsteps pounding behind her.

Amanda was chasing her.

She had to make it to the woods where she could take shelter.

She would take the dangers of the wilderness to the danger of Amanda any time.

As she took another step, her feet sank into murky water. She ignored the moisture that crept up her leg and kept charging forward.

If she could reach the woods, then follow along the roadside, maybe she stood a chance of escaping.

She wasn't sure how big the forest around her was, but it was large. Finley hadn't seen anyone else around them for miles—probably because most of this land was uninhabitable.

"Finley!" Amanda called again as she continued to chase her. "Get back here!"

Another bullet flew.

How could her friend have turned on her like this? How could Amanda think that Finley was responsible for her husband's death?

Grief did all kinds of strange things to people.

Finley darted around a tree and changed directions, hoping to throw Amanda off the trail. As she ran deep into the forest, the putrid scent of rot and decay surrounded her.

As did the mosquitoes. The insects swarmed around her face, and flies buzzed in her ears.

But she continued forward.

Her feet sank into water. Sometimes to her ankles. Sometimes to her knees. The ground beneath the puddles was murky and sticky.

Her loafers suctioned to the mud until she was barefoot.

There was nothing she could do about that now.

Instead, Finley prayed she didn't sink so much that she couldn't get out. That she didn't run into a snake or a bear or an alligator.

Nothing about the situation was ideal.

But she had to keep pressing forward.

Because out here there was no one else to help her . . . no one except God.

I'm sorry I accused You of picking on me . . . because I could really use Your help right now. I know You've allowed me to go through the fire, but I believe good can come out of this situation. But only with Your help. Please . . . I'm begging You, Lord.

As Brandon turned his SUV toward the cabin, a new sound split the air.

A gunshot.

His heart pounded harder.

Finley was in trouble. He was certain of it.

He pulled to the side of the road and cut his engine. He couldn't drive all the way to the cabin. It was too risky. The FBI could be on their way too.

Instead, he hurried from his SUV and began jogging down the road toward the location where Amanda's phone had last pinged.

Colton had called him back several minutes earlier to let him know that the address was for a hunting cabin that belonged to one of Amanda's coworkers.

What was going on inside the cabin?

Part of him didn't want to know. But mostly Brandon prayed that he wasn't too late.

As he got closer to the cabin, he saw the other vehicles there.

Then he realized who it was.

The feds.

Somehow, they'd beat him here.

Probably because Amanda had called in the anonymous tip to let them know Finley was here. He wasn't sure all the reasons why yet, but he felt certain Amanda was the one behind this.

In the end, she'd probably pretend like she was a victim. That Finley had set her up.

"Freeze! Put your hands up!" a deep voice said.

Brandon frowned but did as he was asked.

A moment later, Agent Bills came into view. "What are you doing here?"

"Looking for Finley."

The agent's eyes narrowed. "So, she is here?"

"I don't know. I believe she's being set up."

His eyes narrowed even more. "Or did you come here to help her escape?"

Brandon's shoulders tightened. "It's not like that."

"I'm going to have to ask you to stay where you are."

"I believe Finley is in trouble—that her life is in danger. I need to help her."

"Why would she be in danger?"

"Because her lawyer is actually behind this. She set Finley up. And now she's trying to kill her."

Bills grunted.

Brandon glanced behind Bills and saw the agents swarming the cabin. "Are they inside?"

Bills stared at him a moment, and Brandon wasn't sure if the man was going to answer.

Finally, he said, "No, they're not. But there's evidence a gun was fired, and there are footprints."

Brandon's heart raced faster. "You've got to let me help."

"You can help by staying out of the way—especially until we clear you."

Brandon started to argue, but he knew there was no use. The agent had a gun trained on him.

Brandon glanced at the woods, wondering if Finley was in trouble.

He'd need to plan his next move very carefully.

Just as that thought settled in his mind, he heard gunfire coming from the woods.

Finley . . . was she okay?

He had to find Finley before one of those bullets found her first.

CHAPTER
FORTY-THREE

"I'M GOING to find you, Finley!" Amanda yelled.

Then a bullet split the air.

Finley froze—but only for a moment—before pulling herself out of one of the watery crevices in the woods. Then she nearly collapsed onto the ground. The murky, thick water had sucked the energy out of her.

But she had to keep going. Amanda was close. Too close for comfort.

As she dragged herself to her feet, her heart pounded out of control.

Finley paused behind a large tree and tried to catch her breath.

And to listen.

But she could hardly hear anything over the sound of her own heartbeat.

Although she'd originally decided to try to run parallel to the driveway, she'd somehow lost her sense of direction, and now she didn't know which way was which.

Where was Amanda now?

The woman was out there somewhere. She wouldn't give up now, not with so much at stake. Finley's so-called friend had too much hatred in her heart.

Finley listened again, and that's when she heard sloshing in the water.

Was Amanda wading through some of the miry depths of the swamp?

Or was it someone—or something—else? Maybe a bear? An alligator?

She shivered again as the possibilities filled her mind.

One wrong move, and Finley would be dead.

She still had so much to live for.

Now that Finley knew she'd been set up, as well as who had done it and why, maybe she could go to the FBI. Maybe she truly could be cleared.

First, she had to get out of these woods alive.

She heard more sloshing. But the sound was louder.

Whoever or whatever was in the water was climbing out.

Slowly, Finley edged toward the other side of the tree, trying to remain out of sight.

She glanced over her shoulder, hoping for a glimpse of whoever was out there.

That's when she spotted Amanda.

But her friend no longer looked like the clean-cut, professional lawyer Finley had known.

Now, her curls were wild and frizzy around her face. Her eyes looked just as untamed as the wilderness around them.

And she held that gun in her hands, whipping it around at every sound she heard.

"I know you're out here," Amanda snapped. "You might as well not put this off any longer."

Her words only confirmed to Finley that Amanda planned on killing her.

That meant Finley couldn't let herself be found, no matter what happened.

"Where'd you go, Finley?" Amanda continued, her voice hardened with bitterness. "You know I'm going to find you."

Finley remained perfectly still, not daring to move.

She continued to watch over her shoulder. The moonlight broke through the canopy of trees overhead and shone on Amanda. She had an almost feral look in her eyes as she glanced around, searching for Finley.

Finley's gaze shot to the ground around her. Were there indentations where she'd walked this way?

It was too dark around her to tell. Besides, she

wasn't sure Amanda even had the skills to track her. But Finley didn't like the possibility.

Finally, Amanda walked away from Finley.

But that didn't mean Finley could simply stay here. She had to get out of these woods. She had to find help.

She surveyed the vast nothingness around her.

Finding help would be easier said than done.

———

Brandon held his breath as he waited.

The feds scrambled toward the woods. As they did, Bills looked back at him.

"Stay there!" the man muttered.

Then Bills ran toward the woods as well.

Brandon couldn't stop thinking about the gunfire. Couldn't stop thinking about Finley being hurt.

That's when he made a split-second decision.

When no one was looking, he darted toward the woods.

Just as he reached the trees, he heard Bills yell, "Hey!"

But he didn't stop.

He kept going.

These woods were large.

There were only four FBI agents out here searching. They needed to split up.

He feared the feds would shoot without asking questions. Or that Amanda would shoot and claim self-defense.

So much could go wrong.

He'd take the consequences of disobeying the FBI agent's orders later.

When he was deep into the woods and had lost anyone following him, he paused. He pulled a flashlight from his pocket and shone it on the ground.

This was the general direction Bills had pointed when he'd said he'd seen footprints.

So which direction had those tracks led?

He paused as his light reflected on something in the water.

A set of eyes.

A gator, he realized.

Just one more danger out here.

He veered in the opposite direction.

He kept a steady pace with his flashlight in one hand and his gun in the other as he walked more deeply into the woods. Between the trees. Through puddles. On the lookout for wildlife.

The forest seemed to go still around him, almost as if it were holding its breath, waiting for whatever was going to happen next.

This place was nowhere to play around. He knew the dangers of this area.

But did Finley? Amanda?

He remained quiet and kept his flashlight down as he walked.

If Amanda or even one of the feds saw him, they could fire. Not only that, but he could only assume Amanda had someone working with her. There was no way she could have done all of this on her own.

No, she must have blackmailed some of her clients into doing her dirty work.

Brandon would be no good to Finley if he was injured or killed.

Finley . . . His gut lurched.

He had to find her and make everything right.

Once the FBI knew Amanda was behind this, he and Finley would stand a chance.

That was all that he wanted. A chance.

Brandon wanted to start their new life together. He wanted happy memories as they grew as a couple.

They wanted to have kids. Four of them.

He hadn't believed it when Finley first told him that's how many children she wanted. But he loved the idea.

Amanda was *not* going to ruin their plans.

Brandon paused as he came to a ditch that was almost more of a small canal.

He had to assume that Finley would have headed toward the road—which was the direction he was walking.

That meant he'd need to cross this water.

He lifted a prayer as he started. As he reached the other side, he saw a shadow.

No . . . a person.

He braced himself.

Was it Finley hiding out? The feds?

Or an attacker waiting to strike?

CHAPTER
FORTY-FOUR

FINLEY HEARD FOOTSTEPS. When she peered over her shoulder, she saw the beam of light on the ground.

Shakes consumed her.

Had Amanda circled back around?

It was the only thing that made sense.

Unless Amanda had somehow called backup.

Amanda couldn't have done all of this on her own. That text Finley had read only seemed to confirm that.

That made this situation even more dangerous.

She only wished she'd been able to talk to Brandon. To give him this update.

But she'd been interrupted.

Finley prayed she'd remain unseen.

Then she saw the beam again.

This time, the light hit her face.

Her eyes widened as she realized she was exposed. She braced herself for trouble.

The beam dropped, and footsteps hurried toward her. "Finley?"

That voice . . . was it . . . Brandon?

Or had wishful thinking taken over her logic?

The next instant, he was in front of her.

It *was* him!

"Brandon!" She threw her arms around him as relief washed through her. "You found me."

"I told you I'd always find you," he murmured into her hair. "And I meant it."

She wanted to relish this moment. To pretend she was safe. But . . . that wasn't reality.

She pulled away from him and whispered, "Amanda's still out here. Still looking for me. She's the one who framed me. We've got to get out of here."

Brandon didn't look surprised—he must have figured it out.

He took her hand and glanced around. "Do you know which way she went?"

Finley pointed in the distance. "That way. But I haven't heard anything from her for several minutes. I don't know where she is now or what she's planning."

"We'll get out of here. We'll be careful. But the feds are looking for you too."

Just as they took the first step, Finley heard someone say, "I wouldn't do that if I were you."

———

Brandon froze and slowly turned.

Amanda stood behind them, her gun raised.

"I knew if I waited long enough, I'd finally find you. Now it looks like I've got a twofer." She smirked.

"Amanda . . . you don't want to do this." Brandon kept his voice calm as he pushed Finley behind him.

He knew by the crazy look in Amanda's eyes that she could pull that trigger at any minute.

"I *do* want to do this!" she snapped. "I've been wanting to do this for a long time!"

"You're only going to make things worse for yourself," Brandon told her, praying that maybe he could talk some sense into her—even though part of him knew better.

"No, I'm not," she rushed. "I'm going to tell everyone that you two tried to frame me. All the evidence is there. They'll think this was self-defense."

"You know it's not that easy," Finley said. "Even if the FBI thinks I'm guilty of cybercrimes and treason, no one will believe I tried to kill my best friend in cold blood."

"People will believe anything! You just have to frame it the right way. Now, enough talking. I can't risk anything ruining my plan!" She raised the gun again.

Brandon tensed as he saw her brace herself.

He had no time to think anything through—only to act.

Just as Amanda pulled the trigger, he dove at her.

But was he in time to stop the bullet from hitting Finley?

CHAPTER
FORTY-FIVE

FINLEY HEARD THE GUNSHOT.

Saw Brandon dive toward Amanda.

Heard a scream split the air—her scream.

Brandon collided with Amanda, and they both hit the ground.

Was Brandon . . . okay?

Her heart beat harder.

He wasn't moving.

Finley started to run to him when Amanda raised her head and moaned.

Finley saw she still had the gun in her hand.

"Oh, no, you don't . . ." She lunged at Amanda.

With an almost animal instinct, Finley grabbed the gun and jerked it from Amanda's hands. Then she aimed it at Amanda.

"I promise you I won't hesitate to pull this trigger," Finley growled. "Don't you dare move."

Carefully, Finley sank on the ground beside Brandon.

She reached for his neck, ready to check his pulse.

Before she could, he let out a moan and turned over.

He was okay!

Finley released the breath from her frozen lungs.

Thank God.

"Brandon?" Her voice quivered as doubt remained.

"I'm okay," he croaked. "Don't worry about me."

With one more glance at him, Finley swallowed hard. Then she turned her full attention on Amanda. "I can't believe you did this."

"I don't know what you're talking about." Amanda's expression suddenly changed from maniacal to pleading as she tried to crawl away from them. "Please, don't hurt me."

No way would Finley let Amanda act like a victim here.

"Drop the act," Finley muttered.

Footsteps sounded behind them.

Amanda's men?

Or the feds?

Amanda seemed to hear them also and she rose, her voice shaky. "Anything you want, I'll do it. Just don't hurt me."

"Good try." Brandon pulled himself to his feet

and drew in a ragged breath "But I don't know why you're doing this whole song and dance now."

Suddenly, Amanda's expression shifted again—back into that of a cornered dog ready to fight. "Because if you think this is over, you're wrong. Dead wrong."

"No, you're the one who's dead wrong." Finley saw FBI agents surround them. "It's over, Amanda."

"We'll see about that," Amanda muttered.

"Yes, we will." Finley kept her gaze on Amanda. "How could you do this?"

Amanda didn't answer.

She didn't have to.

Finley had lost her childhood friend a long time ago. She just hadn't known it until tonight.

As the feds took the gun from her, she prayed this was finally all over.

———

The feds led Amanda away, despite the way she screamed and proclaimed her innocence. Apparently, Colton had sent them the evidence they needed to prove Amanda truly was the bad guy here.

Brandon and Finley stood on the edge of the woods—muddy, sweaty, and surrounded by mosquitoes.

But they had no reason to complain.

They were alive. Safe. And Amanda was no longer a threat.

As one of the agents wandered away from them, Brandon turned to Finley, grateful for a brief moment alone. He pulled her into his arms.

She didn't object.

"I'm so sorry I left," she muttered in his ear. "I only wanted what was best for you."

"The two of us being together is what is best for me."

Emotion clouded her voice. "I just hated to think about your life being ruined—"

Brandon shushed her. "You could never ruin my life. Don't think like that."

"I love you so much." Finley held him tighter.

"I love you too." He kissed her forehead and let his lips linger there a long time, never wanting to let go.

When a commotion sounded around them, he had no choice but to pull away. But he kept one arm around Finley as they both turned to watch Amanda being questioned.

Brandon knew he and Finley weren't in the clear yet either. They'd be questioned, probably extensively. That was okay. He truly believed everyone would see the truth of the matter now.

Colton excused himself from a conversation with one of feds and strode toward Finley and Brandon. He'd gotten here just in time.

He paused and observed them both a moment. "I'm glad you're okay."

"Me too," Brandon murmured. "Thanks for coming."

"Of course." Colton turned to Finley. "How are you holding up?"

"As well as can be expected." Finley huddled closer to Brandon. "I still can't believe my friend did this to me."

"She needed someone to blame for her husband's suicide, and you seemed like the best option." Colton shrugged as if the whole scenario didn't make sense to him either.

"I guess so." A frown tugged at Finley's lips. "But it all just seems so extreme."

"I agree." Brandon's arm tightened around her.

"How was she following us? Especially when we went to see Ryan?"

"She was blackmailing different people she saved from prison in the past. Threatening that she could put them behind bars if they didn't do exactly what she wanted. She had some of the best criminals at her disposal doing this."

"So, somehow those people were tracking us?"

"Possibly. I have to wonder if Amanda threw a tracker into your purse or somewhere else also. Otherwise, it was probably because she overheard our plans. She put herself in the prime position for this."

Just then, Agent Bills stepped toward them, his gaze on Finley. Brandon felt himself tense again as worst-case scenarios tried to play out in his mind.

He closed his eyes and lifted a prayer—for wisdom, for comfort, for people's eyes to be opened.

As he said amen, a peace beyond understanding washed over him.

He and Finley would explain what happened. If the justice system worked the way it was supposed to, Finley wouldn't be charged with these crimes.

And Amanda would be going away for a very long time.

He had to trust that was going to be the case.

EPILOGUE

ONE WEEK LATER

WITH HER BRIDESMAIDS SURROUNDING HER, Finley glanced in the mirror at the simple white dress she wore and grinned.

This wasn't her original wedding gown. That one had been ruined when she'd been arrested.

She'd had the opportunity to wear a similar one today, but knew that doing so would bring back too many bad memories.

So she'd started fresh.

She'd found a different gown—this one beautiful in its own way with its strapless top and billowy train.

And her bouquet . . . it was made of fresh-cut roses.

Which was what she'd wanted in the first place.

Classic red roses.

They weren't from the most expensive florist in

the area, but they were just as beautiful and amazingly fragrant.

This ceremony was smaller. She and Brandon had only invited their closest friends.

Everything had gone according to plan so far. The refrigerator hadn't broken down. The weather was beautiful.

The danger was behind them.

Carter Denver had still been available to play the guitar, but they'd changed the song set.

This time, Finley would walk down the aisle to "I See the Light."

Tangled had been the last musical she and her mom had seen together before her mom had passed. Playing the song right now seemed like a great homage to her parents.

Thankfully, the charges against Finley had been dropped, and now Amanda was the one being held for trial.

Finley still couldn't believe all the trouble her so-called friend had gone through in order to exact revenge. But grief had done a horrible number on her. She'd wanted someone else to suffer just as she had.

She, Brandon, and the other members of the team had been diving deep as they looked for answers. But the truth could be found at a much shallower place instead.

That extra evidence that the prosecution had

found? Amanda had fabricated that fact to keep Finley's apprehension raised. And those civil suits filed against Finley had now been transferred to Amanda.

The woman had a long road ahead of her.

Finley wanted to hate her. But she couldn't.

Instead, she felt sorry for the woman she'd considered a friend for so long.

But today wasn't the day to think about those things.

Today was a day to celebrate.

"Are you ready for this?" Taryn appeared in the doorway of the classroom where Finley was getting ready.

"I've been ready."

The two women shared a smile.

A moment later, Finley left the classroom, walked down the hallway and into the foyer. As the doors to the sanctuary opened, her song began to play. Tears pricked her eyes as the enormity of this moment hit her.

If only her mom and dad could be here to see it . . . but somehow, she knew they were both here in spirit.

She glanced at the end of the aisle and saw Brandon standing on the stage with a grin on his face.

He looked so incredibly handsome. Finley was so extremely blessed to have him in her life.

She couldn't take her eyes off him as she walked down the aisle.

This time, no one interrupted them.

Everything was perfect.

It was as if this day were meant to be their special day all along.

As soon as Finley reached Brandon, she handed her bouquet to Katie Logan, her maid of honor. Then Brandon took her hands into his.

Everything seemed like a wonderful, blissful blur as they said their vows and Pastor Jack Wilson pronounced them husband and wife.

Cheers filled the room, and Finley couldn't help but laugh.

She felt just as happy and relieved as they did.

Then Pastor Jack said, "You may kiss your bride."

Brandon leaned toward Finley but paused before their lips met.

"I'm the luckiest guy in the whole world," he murmured. "You know that?"

"Funny because I was thinking that I was the luckiest girl in the whole world."

"Then I guess we're blessed that we found each other."

He grinned before his lips covered hers.

Another round of cheers sounded around them.

They wouldn't be headed to the Maldives for their honeymoon. Instead, they would head north to Cape Corral, a community on the northern end of the

Outer Banks. Wild horses roamed there, and there were no paved streets.

It sounded like the perfect getaway.

Maybe things were finally looking up.

~~~

Thank you so much for reading *Deceptive Shallows*. If you enjoyed this book, please consider leaving a review.

Stayed tuned for *Secret Shores*, coming next!

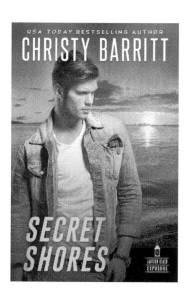

ALSO BY CHRISTY BARRITT:

OTHER BOOKS IN THE LANTERN BEACH SERIES:

LANTERN BEACH MYSTERIES

Hidden Currents

You can take the detective out of the investigation, but you can't take the investigator out of the detective. A notorious gang puts a bounty on Detective Lady Matthews's head after she takes down their leader, leaving her no choice but to hide until she can testify at trial. But her temporary home across the country on a remote North Carolina island isn't as peaceful as she initially thinks. Living under the new identity of Cassidy Livingston, she struggles to keep her investigative skills tucked away, especially after a body washes ashore. When local police bungle the murder investigation, she can't resist stepping in. But Cassidy is supposed to be keeping a low profile. One wrong move could lead to both her discovery and her demise. Can she bring justice to the island . . . or will the hidden currents surrounding her pull her under for good?

Flood Watch

The tide is high, and so is the danger on Lantern Beach. Still in hiding after infiltrating a dangerous gang, Cassidy Livingston just has to make it a few more months before she can testify at trial and resume her old life. But trouble keeps finding her, and Cassidy is pulled into a local investigation after a man mysteriously disappears from the island she now calls home. A recurring nightmare from her time undercover only muddies things, as does a visit from the parents of her handsome ex-Navy SEAL neighbor. When a friend's life is threatened, Cassidy must make choices that put her on the verge of blowing her cover. With a flood watch on her emotions and her life in a tangle, will Cassidy find the truth? Or will her past finally drown her?

Storm Surge

A storm is brewing hundreds of miles away, but its effects are devastating even from afar. Laid-back, loose, and light: that's Cassidy Livingston's new motto. But when a makeshift boat with a bloody cloth inside washes ashore near her oceanfront home, her detective instincts shift into gear . . . again. Seeking clues isn't the only thing on her mind—romance is heating up with next-door neighbor and former Navy SEAL Ty Chambers as well. Her heart wants the love and stability she's longed for her entire life. But her hidden identity only leads to a tidal wave of turbulence. As more answers emerge about the boat, the danger around her rises, creating a treacherous swell that threatens to reveal her past. Can Cassidy mind her own business, or will the storm surge of violence and corruption that has washed ashore on Lantern Beach leave her life in wreckage?

Dangerous Waters

Danger lurks on the horizon, leaving only two choices: find shelter or flee. Cassidy Livingston's new identity has begun to feel as comfortable as her favorite sweater. She's been tucked away on Lantern Beach for weeks, waiting to testify against a deadly gang, and is settling in to a new life she wants to last forever. When she thinks she spots someone malevolent from her past, panic swells inside her. If an enemy has found her, Cassidy won't be the only one who's a target. Everyone she's come to love will also be at risk. Dangerous waters threaten to pull her into an overpowering chasm she may never escape. Can Cassidy survive what lies ahead? Or has the tide fatally turned against her?

Perilous Riptide

Just when the current seems safer, an unseen

danger emerges and threatens to destroy everything. When Cassidy Livingston finds a journal hidden deep in the recesses of her ice cream truck, her curiosity kicks into high gear. Islanders suspect that Elsa, the journal's owner, didn't die accidentally. Her final entry indicates their suspicions might be correct and that what Elsa observed on her final night may have led to her demise. Against the advice of Ty Chambers, her former Navy SEAL boyfriend, Cassidy taps into her detective skills and hunts for answers. But her search only leads to a skeletal body and trouble for both of them. As helplessness threatens to drown her, Cassidy is desperate to turn back time. Can Cassidy find what she needs to navigate the perilous situation? Or will the riptide surrounding her threaten everyone and everything Cassidy loves?

Deadly Undertow

The current's fatal pull is powerful, but so is one detective's will to live. When someone from Cassidy Livingston's past shows up on Lantern Beach and warns her of impending peril, opposing currents collide, threatening to drag her under. Running would be easy. But leaving would break her heart. Cassidy must decipher between the truth and lies, between reality and deception. Even more importantly, she must decide whom to trust and whom to fear. Her life depends on it. As danger rises and answers surface, everything Cassidy thought she knew is tested. In order to survive, Cassidy must take drastic measures and end the battle against the ruthless gang DH-7 once and for all. But if her final mission fails, the consequences will be as deadly as the raging undertow.

LANTERN BEACH ROMANTIC SUSPENSE

Tides of Deception
Change has come to Lantern Beach: a new police chief, a new season, and . . . a new romance? Austin Brooks has loved Skye Lavinia from the moment they met, but the walls she keeps around her seem impenetrable. Skye knows Austin is the best thing to ever happen to her. Yet she also knows that if he learns the truth about her past, he'd be a fool not to run. A chance encounter brings secrets bubbling to the surface, and danger soon follows. Are the life-threatening events plaguing them really accidents . . . or is someone trying to send a deadly message? With the tides on Lantern Beach come deception and lies. One question remains—who will be swept away as the water shifts? And will it bring the end for Austin and Skye, or merely the beginning?

Shadow of Intrigue
For her entire life, Lisa Garth has felt like a supporting character in the drama of life. The desig-

nation never bothered her—until now. Lantern Beach, where she's settled and runs a popular restaurant, has boarded up for the season. The slower pace leaves her with too much time alone. Braden Dillinger came to Lantern Beach to try to heal. The former Special Forces officer returned from battle with invisible scars and diminished hope. But his recovery is hampered by the fact that an unknown enemy is trying to kill him. From the moment Lisa and Braden meet, danger ignites around them, and both are drawn into a web of intrigue that turns their lives upside down. As shadows creep in, will Lisa and Braden be able to shine a light on the peril around them? Or will the encroaching darkness turn their worst nightmares into reality?

Storm of Doubt

A pastor who's lost faith in God. A romance writer who's lost faith in love. A faceless man with a deadly obsession. Nothing has felt right in Pastor Jack Wilson's world since his wife died two years ago. He hoped coming to Lantern Beach might help soothe the ragged edges of his soul. Instead, he feels more alone than ever. Novelist Juliette Grace came to the island to hide away. Though her professional life has never been better, her personal life has imploded. Her husband left her and a stalker's threats have grown more and more dangerous. When Jack saves Juliette from an attack, he sees the terror in her gaze and knows he must protect her. But when danger strikes again, will Jack be able to keep her safe? Or will the approaching storm prove too strong to withstand?

Winds of Danger

Wes O'Neill is perfectly content to hang with his friends and enjoy island life on Lantern Beach. Something begins to change inside him when Paige Henderson sweeps into his life. But the beautiful newcomer is hiding painful secrets beneath her cheerful facade. Police dispatcher Paige Henderson came to Lantern Beach riddled with guilt and uncertainties after the fallout of a bad relationship. When she meets Wes, she begins to open up to the possibility of love again. But there's something Wes isn't telling her—something that could change everything. As the winds shift, doubts seep into Paige's mind. Can Paige and Wes trust each other, even as the currents work against them? Or is trouble from the past too much to overcome?

Rains of Remorse

A stranger invades her home, leaving Rebecca Jarvis terrified. Above all, she must protect the baby growing inside her. Since her estranged husband died suspiciously six months earlier, Rebecca has been determined to depend on no one but herself. Her chivalrous new neighbor appears to be an answer to prayer. But who is Levi Stoneman really? Rebecca wants to believe he can help her, but she can't ignore her instincts. As danger closes in, both Rebecca and Levi must figure out whom they can trust. With Rebecca's baby coming soon, there's no time to waste. Can the truth prevail . . . or will remorse overpower the best of intentions?

Torrents of Fear

The woman lingering in the crowd can't be Allison . . . can she? Because Allison was pronounced dead six years ago. Musician Carter Denver knows only one person who's capable of helping him find answers: Sadie Thompson, his estranged best friend and someone who also knew Allison. He needs to know if he's losing his mind or if Allison could have survived her car accident. Could Allison really be alive? If so, why is she trying to harm Carter and Sadie? As the two try to find answers, can Sadie keep her feelings for Carter hidden? Could he ever care for her, or is the man of her dreams still in love with the woman now causing his nightmares?

LANTERN BEACH PD

On the Lookout

A runaway woman. A dead body. A mysterious compound. When Cassidy Chambers accepted the job as police chief on Lantern Beach, she knew the island had its secrets. But a suspicious death with potentially far-reaching implications will test all her skills—and threaten to reveal her true identity. Cassidy enlists the help of her husband, former Navy SEAL Ty Chambers. As they dig for answers, both uncover parts of their pasts that are best left buried. Not everything is as it seems, and they must figure out if their John Doe is connected to the secretive group that has moved onto the island. As facts materialize, danger on the island grows. Can Cassidy and Ty discover the truth about the shadowy crimes in their cozy community? Or has darkness permanently invaded their beloved Lantern Beach?

Attempt to Locate

A fun girls' night out turns into a nightmare when armed robbers barge into the store where Cassidy and her friends are shopping. As the situation escalates and the men escape, a massive manhunt launches on Lantern Beach to apprehend the dangerous trio. In the midst of the chaos, a potential foe asks for Cassidy's help. He needs to find his sister who fled from the secretive Gilead's Cove community on the island. But the more Cassidy learns about the seemingly untouchable group, the more her unease grows. The pressure to solve both cases continues to mount. But as the gravity of the situation rises, so does the danger. Cassidy is determined to protect the island and break up the cult . . . but doing so might cost her everything.

First Degree Murder

Police Chief Cassidy Chambers longs for a break from the recent crimes plaguing Lantern Beach. She simply wants to enjoy her friends' upcoming wedding, to prepare for the busy tourist season about to slam the island, and to gather all the dirt she can on the suspicious community that's invaded the town. But trouble explodes on the island, sending residents—including Cassidy—into a squall of uneasiness. Cassidy may have more than one enemy plotting her demise, and the collateral damage seems unthinkable. As the temperature rises, so does the pressure to find answers. Someone is determined that Lantern Beach would be better off without their new police chief. And for Cassidy, one wrong move could mean certain death.

Dead on Arrival

With a highly charged local election consuming the community, Police Chief Cassidy Chambers braces herself for a challenging day of breaking up petty conflicts and tamping down high emotions. But when widespread food poisoning spreads among potential voters across the island, Cassidy smells something rotten in the air. As Cassidy examines every possibility to uncover what's going on, local enigma Anthony Gilead again comes on her radar. The man is running for mayor and his cult-like following is growing at an alarming rate. Cassidy feels certain he has a spy embedded in her inner circle. The problem is that her pool of suspects gets deeper every day. Can Cassidy get to the bottom of what's eating away at her peaceful island home? Will voters turn out despite the outbreak of illness plaguing their tranquil town? And the even bigger question: Has darkness come to stay on Lantern Beach?

Plan of Action

A missing Navy SEAL. Danger at the boiling point. The ultimate showdown. When Police Chief Cassidy Chambers' husband, Ty, disappears, her world is turned upside down. His truck is discovered with blood inside, crashed in a ditch on Lantern Beach, but he's nowhere to be found. As they launch a manhunt to find him, Cassidy discovers that someone on the island has a deadly obsession with Ty. Meanwhile, Gilead's Cove seems to be imploding. As danger heightens, federal law enforcement officials are called in. The cult's growing threat could lead to the pinnacle standoff of good versus evil. A clear plan of action is needed or the results will be devastating. Will Cassidy find Ty in time, or will she face a gut-wrenching loss? Will Anthony Gilead finally be unmasked for who he really is and be brought to justice? Hundreds of innocent lives are at stake . . . and not everyone will come out alive.

LANTERN BEACH ESCAPE

Afterglow

What if you married someone, only to discover that she was suspected of killing her former fiancé? While on their honeymoon, Grayson and Rachel Stewart are confronted with dark details of Rachel's past. As more facts begin emerging, their new marriage is thrown into a tailspin. The newlyweds must figure out how to move forward . . . and Grayson must figure out if he married a killer.

LANTERN BEACH BLACKOUT

Dark Water

Colton Locke can't forget the black op that went terribly wrong. Desperate for a new start, he moves to Lantern Beach, North Carolina, and forms Blackout, a private security firm. Despite his hero status, he can't erase the mistakes he's made. For the past year, Elise Oliver hasn't been able to shake the feeling that there's more to her husband's death than she was told. When she finds a hidden box of his personal possessions, more questions—and suspicions—arise. The only person she trusts to help her is her husband's best friend, Colton Locke. Someone wants Elise dead. Is it because she knows too much? Or is it to keep her from finding the truth? The Blackout team must uncover dark secrets hiding beneath seemingly still waters. But those very secrets might just tear the team apart.

Safe Harbor

Guilt over past mistakes haunts former Navy SEAL Dez Rodriguez. When he's asked to guard a pop star during a music festival on Lantern Beach, he's all set for what he hopes is a breezy assignment. Bree hasn't found fame to be nearly as fulfilling as she dreamed. Instead, she's more like a carefully crafted character living out a pre-scripted story. When a stalker's threats become deadly, her life—and career—are turned upside down. From the start, Bree sees her temporary bodyguard as a player, and Dez sees Bree as a spoiled rich girl. But when they're thrown together in a fight for survival, both must learn to trust. Can Dez protect Bree—and his carefully guarded heart? Or will their safe harbor ultimately become their death trap?

Ripple Effect

Griff McIntyre never expected his ex-wife and three-year-old daughter to come to Lantern Beach. After an abduction attempt, they're desperate for safety. Now Griff's not letting either of them out of his sight. Bethany knows Griff is the only one who can protect them, despite the fact that he broke her heart. But she'll do anything to keep her daughter safe—even if it means playing nicely with a man she can't stand. As peril ripples through their lives, Griff and Bethany must work together to protect their daughter. But an unseen enemy wants something from them . . . and will stop at nothing to get it. When disaster strikes, can Griff keep his family safe? Or will past mistakes bring the ultimate failure?

Rising Tide

Benjamin James knows there's a traitor within his former command. The rest of his team might even think it's him. As danger closes in, he must clear himself and stop a deadly plot by a dangerous terrorist group. All CJ Compton wanted was a new start after her career ended under suspicion. Working as the house manager for private security group Blackout seems perfect. But there's more trouble here than what she left behind. As the tide rushes in, the stakes continue to rise. If the Blackout team fails, it's not just Lantern Beach at stake—it's the whole country. Can Benjamin and CJ overcome their differences and work together to find the truth?

LANTERN BEACH GUARDIANS

Hide and Seek

During a turbulent storm, a child is found on the

*beach, washed up from the ocean. Making matters worse—
the girl can't speak.* Lantern Beach Police Chief Cassidy
Chambers can feel the danger lurking around them.
As more mysterious incidents happen on the island,
Cassidy fears each crime is somehow connected to
this child—a child no one has reported missing.
Cassidy knows the girl's life depends on finding
answers. With the help of her husband, Ty, a former
Navy SEAL, she scrambles to discover what exactly
is going on. Someone appears to be playing a deadly
version of hide-and-seek—and using the girl as a
pawn. But what will happen when the game finally
ends? *Hide and Seek is the first book in a three book
series. Though the main storyline of each book will
be wrapped up at the end, some plot lines will not be
resolved until the end of book three.*

Shock and Awe

They thought the worst was over—but they were
wrong.When Police Chief Cassidy Chambers arrives
at a grisly crime scene, she's shocked at where the
evidence leads. Then the threats start coming. Threats
against her. Threats that could upend her life.As
more clues are uncovered, a sinister plot is revealed,
and Cassidy fears the little girl in her care may be
tangled in a deadly scheme. Cassidy and her
husband, Ty, will do anything to protect the child,
each other, and the island. But what happens when
they might not be able to save all three?

Safe and Sound

A call for help draws Police Chief Cassidy Chambers deep into a wooded, isolated area on Lantern Beach. What she finds shakes her to the core—a friend is bleeding out, and his last words before dying are: They know. Figuring out who killed her friend and what his final words meant becomes Cassidy's mission. Have members of the notorious gang that placed a bounty on her head discovered her new life? Or is someone else trying to teach her a twisted lesson? Elements from past investigations surface and threaten more than one person's safety. Cassidy and her husband, Ty, must make sense of the deadly secrets that unfold at every turn. If not, the life they've built together might come to a permanent end.

LANTERN BEACH BLACKOUT: THE NEW RECRUITS

Rocco

Former Navy SEAL and new Blackout recruit Rocco Foster is on a simple in and out mission. But the operation turns complicated when an unsuspecting woman wanders into the line of fire. Peyton Ellison's life mission is to sprinkle happiness on those around her. When a cupcake delivery turns into a fight for survival, she must trust her rescuer—a handsome stranger—to keep her safe. Rocco is determined to figure out why someone is targeting Peyton. First, he must keep the intriguing woman safe and earn her trust. But threats continue to pummel them as incriminating evidence emerges and pits them against each other. With time running out, the two must set aside both their growing attraction and their doubts about each other in order to work together. But the perilous facts they discover leave them wondering what exactly the truth is . . . and if the truth can be trusted.

Axel

Women are missing. Private security firm Blackout must find them before another victim disappears. Axel Hendrix likes to live on the edge. That's why being a Navy SEAL suited him so well. But after his last mission, he cut his losses and joined Blackout instead. His team's latest case involves an undercover investigation on Lantern Beach. Olivia Rollins came to the island to escape her problems—and danger. When trouble from her past shows up in town, she impulsively blurts she's engaged to Axel, the womanizing man she's seen while waitressing. Now, she may not be the only one in danger. So could Axel. Axel knows Olivia might be his chance to find answers and that acting like her fiancé is the perfect cover for his latest assignment. But he doesn't like throwing Olivia into the middle of such a dangerous situation. Nor is he comfortable with the feelings she stirs inside him. With Olivia's life—as well as both their hearts—on the line, Axel must uncover the truth and stop an evil plan before more lives are destroyed.

Beckett

When the daughter of a federal judge is abducted, private security firm Blackout must find her. Psychologist Samantha Reynolds doesn't know why someone is targeting her. Even after a risky mission to save her, danger still lingers. She's determined to use her insights into the human mind to help decode the deadly clues being left in the wake of her rescue. Former Navy SEAL Beckett Jones needs to figure out who's responsible for the crimes hounding Sami. He's not sure why he's so protective of the woman he rescued, but he'll do anything to keep her safe—even if it means risking his heart. As the body count rises, there's no room for error. Beckett and Sami must both tear down the careful walls they've built around themselves in order to survive. If they don't figure out who's responsible, the madman will continue his death spree . . . and one of them might be next.

Gabe

When former Navy SEAL and current Blackout operative Gabe Michaels is almost killed in a hit-and-run, the aftermath completely upends his life. He's no longer safe—and he's not the only one. Dr.

Autumn Spenser came to Lantern Beach to start fresh. But while treating Gabe after his accident, she senses there's more to what happened to him than meets the eye. When she digs deeper into his past, she never expects to be drawn into a deadly dilemma. Gabe has been infatuated with the pretty doctor since the day they met. Now, can he keep her from harm? Could someone out of his league ever return his feelings or will her past hurts keep them apart? As danger continues to pummel them, Gabe and Autumn are thrown together in a quest to find answers. More important than their growing attraction, they must stay alive long enough to stop the person desperate to destroy them.

LANTERN BEACH MAYDAY

Run Aground

A dead captain on a luxury yacht leads to a tumultuous seafaring journey . . . Med student Kenzie Anderson, tired of letting others chart her future, accepts a job as second steward aboard Almost Paradise. But when she finds the captain dead before the charter even begins, her plans seem to capsize. Jimmy James Gamble senses something vulnerable and slightly naive about Kenzie when he finds her on the docks. Realizing danger may still be lingering close, he uses his hidden skills to earn a place on the charter. But being there causes him to risk everything—especially as more suspicious incidents occur. As they set out to sea, Kenzie and Jimmy James both wonder if they're in over their heads. They must figure out how to stop a killer before anyone onboard is hurt . . . otherwise, both their futures might just run aground.

Dead Reckoning

A yachtie fears for her life when she's the only witness to a murder . . . Kenzie Anderson knows what she saw at the harbor—a woman strangled and pushed overboard. But there's no proof of a crime . . . only her word. Jimmy James Gamble believes Kenzie, even if no one else does. As he senses the danger in the air, all he wants is to keep her away from any more trouble—especially after their last charter. Either Kenzie or the yacht they're working on seem to be a magnet for murder and mayhem. Someone is willing to kill to get what he wants—and will do so again if necessary. Can Jimmy James and Kenzie navigate these unfamiliar waters? Or will relying on dead reckoning lead them to their deaths?

Tipping Point

Awakening in a boat surrounded by nothing but water, a yachtie has no doubt someone wants her dead. Kenzie Anderson is determined not to let anyone scare her away from completing the charter season—even with the threats on her life. The only person she can trust is Captain Jimmy James Gamble, despite their tumultuous relationship. Kenzie and Jimmy James both suspect turbulent currents rush beneath the tranquil surface aboard the luxury yacht Almost Paradise. Secrets seem to abound, each one increasing the tension aboard the boat. As answers rise to the surface, neither Kenzie nor Jimmy James is prepared for what they find. Have they both reached their tipping points? Their adversaries want nothing more than to make Kenzie disappear . . . forever. It may be too late for a mayday call.

LANTERN BEACH CHRISTMAS

Silent Night

Catch up with your favorite Lantern Beach characters as they come together to help the town's beloved police chief. On the night before Christmas Eve, as she begins her maternity leave, Lantern Beach Police Chief Cassidy Chambers disappears. Suspecting foul play, law enforcement officers combine forces with the Blackout Security team and island residents to find her. Despite a snowstorm in his path, Cassidy's husband, Ty, desperately tries to return home in time to save her. With his wife's and baby's lives on the line, he needs a Christmas miracle. Will the tightknit community of Lantern Beach be able to rescue their beloved police chief in time? Or will Cassidy's cries for help be met only with silence?

LANTERN BEACH BLACKOUT: DANGER RISING

Brandon

Physically he's protecting her. But emotionally she's never felt more exposed. The last person tech heiress Finley Cooper ever wanted to see again was Brandon Hale. Two years ago, Brandon shattered her heart. Now Finley needs protection, and, against her wishes, Brandon is assigned the job. Even worse, they must pretend to be a couple in order to find answers. Brandon, a former Navy SEAL, met Finley while on an undercover assignment in Ecuador. But he broke her trust, and now he doesn't blame Finley for hating him. As a new Blackout operative, Brandon's first assignment throws him into Finley's life 24/7. Someone wants her dead, and it's clear this person won't stop until that mission is accomplished. To keep her safe, Brandon must regain Finley's trust. Can he convince her she's more than a job to him? Or will peril permanently silence them?

Dylan

His job is to protect her. The trouble is . . . she doesn't want protection. Former Navy SEAL Dylan Granger's new assignment requires him to use both his tactical abilities and his acting skills. Hired by Katie Logan's father, his job is to protect the gutsy university professor while concealing his identity. To maintain his cover, he takes the unassuming role of her new assistant. Katie—a disgraced reporter—has stumbled upon a lead she can't ignore. Now it's clear someone is targeting her, but she refuses to back down. Her handsome new assistant is a welcome distraction from the chaos. But Dylan's skillset goes way beyond his job description, and Katie begins to suspect there's more to Dylan than he's letting on. Dylan's mission can't be disclosed—not if he wants to keep Katie safe. But as his feelings for her grow and the danger increases, keeping his secret becomes more of a challenge than he ever imagined. With innocent lives on the line, Dylan must choose between protecting Katie or savings others.

Maddox

He's on the case . . . and she's his prime suspect. Classified technology is missing, a delivery driver is dead, and former Navy SEAL Maddox King must find the culprits before a dangerous plan is enacted. To find answers, the Blackout agent must go undercover as a maintenance man at millionaire Seymore Whitlock's estate. While there, he sets his sights on Whitlock's personal assistant, Taryn Parsons, a woman who has everything to gain and nothing to lose. Six months ago, Whitlock plucked Taryn out of obscurity to become his caretaker. But with deadly incidents haunting the estate, Taryn doesn't know who she can trust—including the new maintenance man who is both intriguing . . . and unnerving. The stakes continue to escalate, and Maddox is running out of time to find answers. With the body count rising along with his list of suspects, this assignment may be his most challenging yet . . . for both his skillset and his heart.

Titus

She shattered his heart once. Can he set her betrayal aside for the sake of his country? The last person Titus Armstrong wants to join forces with is the woman who dumped him for his brother, Alex. But Presley Lennox is Blackout's best chance at infiltrating a dangerous organization known as The System and finding out more about their deadly plans. Presley Lennox wants out—of both an abusive relationship and the radical group she's become entangled with because of Alex. When Titus reappears in her life, he's like an answer to prayer—until he asks her to dive deeper into the very life she's been trying to escape. A dangerous plan is brewing that could destroy thousands of lives. Titus and Presley may be the only ones who can stop what's about to be unleashed. Failure would mean certain chaos . . . not only for them but for their nation.

BEACH BOUND BOOKS AND BEANS MYSTERIES

Bound by Murder

When widow Talitha Robinson buys an old store on the boardwalk in Lantern Beach, North Carolina, she's in for a surprise . . . or several. She plans to renovate the space and open Beach Bound Books and Beans, but never expects to find a decades-old skeleton hidden inside one of the walls. As word of the discovery spreads across the island, strange occurrences begin to occur around her. It soon becomes clear someone still knows something about the dead person—something they don't want discovered. Thankfully, former police chief and current mayor Mac MacArthur seems just as eager to unravel the mystery behind the skeletal remains as Tali. But as the two bind together to solve the case, a devastating secret is revealed. Will their newfound friendship come unglued before they find the answers to the past? Or will their blooming relationship die like the man hidden in the wall?Bound by Murder is book 1 in a four book series of novellas. Though the main mystery is resolved, there are threads that will continue throughout the entire series.

Bound by Disaster

Talitha Robinson is knee-deep in renovations as she prepares to open her new bookstore when a body washes ashore on Lantern Beach. While news of the suspicious death surges across the island, a stranger comes knocking on Tali's door, begging her to endorse his unfinished suspense novel. Unable to dissuade the author, Tali is left holding his manuscript in her hands. But she has no idea of the peril written on its pages. Mac MacArthur has kept his distance from Tali since they uncovered a shocking connection about their pasts. But when someone begins to act out the murderous scenes from the book, one victim at a time, Mac's protective instincts override his decision to stay away. As danger escalates, Mac and Tali must manage their conflicting feelings as they work together to stop this killer . . . before the last chapter is written.

Bound by Mystery

Talitha Robinson is well on her way to completing renovations for her new bookstore, Beach Bound Books and Beans, in Lantern Beach, North Carolina. But when she hosts a friendly meet-and-greet with bookstore owners from nearby islands, the progress she's making comes to a deadly end. Someone is backstabbed—literally—right under Tali's nose. To make matters worse, Tali's fingerprints are all over the murder weapon and a neighbor claims to have seen Tali commit the crime. Mac MacArthur knows Tali isn't the type to hurt anyone, but it doesn't take a former police chief to figure out things don't look good for her. The two work together to read between the lines and decipher the truth before Tali gets locked away for crimes she didn't commit. As more evidence stacks up, it becomes clear that someone wants to take Tali out of the story. For good.

Bound by Trouble

With the grand opening of Beach Bound Books and Beans, Tali Robinson's dreams are finally coming true. She hopes to now put the past behind her and start a new chapter. When a suspicious stranger mysteriously shows up at her celebration, her hopes disappear faster than a bestseller at a book signing.Mac MacArthur is ready to solidify his relationship with Tali. But mending their differences is easier said than done. Then someone sets their sights on Tali—and wants to put her out of print . . . permanently. With trouble brewing, Tali and Mac have no choice but to dive into the chaos of the past. However, as more answers are revealed, the danger increases. The truth will come at a great cost . . . one that will bind them together or drive them apart.

Bound by Mayhem

As cast and crew members prepare for Lantern Beach's first annual Christmas play, catastrophe strikes. Abby Mendez, the director and brainchild behind the play, never shows up for a dress rehearsal. Threats emerge, and it becomes clear that not everyone on the island feels the Christmas spirit. With dangerous encounters and ghostly disappearing acts threatening not only the play but also the safety of Lantern Beach residents, former police chief Mac MacArthur and Abby's friend Tali Robinson jump in to help. The stakes rise as the perpetrator continues to haunt Abby's past, torment her present, and threaten her future. When it seems all hope is nearly lost, can the people of Lantern Beach work together to save the play? Or will this phantom scrooge steal the final act?

ABOUT THE AUTHOR

USA Today has called Christy Barritt's books "scary, funny, passionate, and quirky."

Christy writes both mystery and romantic suspense novels that are clean with underlying messages of faith. Her books have sold more than four million copies and have won the Daphne du Maurier Award for Excellence in Suspense and Mystery, have been twice nominated for the Romantic Times Reviewers' Choice Award, and have finaled for both a Carol Award and Foreword Magazine's Book of the Year.

She is married to her Prince Charming, a man who thinks she's hilarious—but only when she's not trying to be. Christy is a self-proclaimed klutz, an avid music lover who's known for spontaneously bursting into song, and a road trip aficionado.

When she's not working or spending time with her family, she enjoys singing, playing the guitar, and exploring small, unsuspecting towns where people have no idea how accident-prone she is.

Find Christy online at:
www.christybarritt.com
www.facebook.com/christybarritt
www.twitter.com/cbarritt

Sign up for Christy's newsletter to get information on all of her latest releases here: **www.christybarritt. com/newsletter-sign-up/**

📘 facebook.com / AuthorChristyBarritt
🐦 twitter.com / christybarritt
📷 instagram.com / cebarritt

Made in the USA
Middletown, DE
27 November 2023